Starting
From
Zero

Starting From Zero

Rom Wills

Wills Publishing

Starting From Zero

ISBN-13: 978-0615883328
ISBN-10: 061588332X

To my sons.

BOOK I

DESCENT

Twenty-Four

Saturday night. Party at Joe's. I've been waiting for this party all week, especially after all the overtime I put into work as a paralegal. The week is over though. Time to party. I shouldn't complain about work. I do get paid well. I have my own place in Northwest, DC. I have a nice car. Not bad for a young Black man in the late 1990's.

I'm well fed. Ha ha. 'Well-fed.' What an understatement. I'm tipping the scales at 240. My cheeks are chubby, but my haircut is tight. The women don't seem to complain. At most people think that I'm a bodybuilder though I've never set foot in a gym. Ah who cares? The phone's ringing. I hope it isn't Jo. I don't feel like dealing with her. "Hello."

"Steve, what's up baby? You coming over tonight?"

Here we go. "Hi Jo. No, I'm not coming over tonight. I didn't tell you that I was coming over tonight. Therefore, there is no reason for me to come over tonight."

"Why not?"

"Because I'm doing something else."

"What?"

"It's not your concern."

"Steve we haven't got together in a couple of weeks. I miss you. I need you. I lo...like being with you."

"Look, I'll talk to you later."

"Why don't you stop by after you finish whatever it is you're doing? You're probably going out with some girl. How come you never take me out?"

"Because we're not like that." I hate when she talks like this.

"You're the one who doesn't want to be like that. You know I want more."

"Look, I'm busy. I have to go. Later." I hang up the phone.

Women! What happened to the good ol' days when they would just sit back and be quiet? Whatever. It's time to get ready.

I love getting ready for parties or dates. First I take a long shower. I towel off and slowly put cocoa butter lotion all over my body. Women talk about you if you have ashy skin. Then I put on the deodorant and the talcum powder. This is DC. I do all this while listening to some jazz. I throw on my socks, my black boxer briefs, and wife beater.

10

My jeans are starting to get a little tight. Dag, they're already size 40. I get any bigger and I'm going to have to go to a big and tall men's shop. Good thing I get paid. I can afford a tent to wear around me if need be. Maybe I'll join a gym. Then again maybe not.

I put on a polo shirt. Some cologne too!

Yeah boy, I look good in the mirror. Just have to brush my hair. Make sure the waves are tight. I grab my jacket. I call the fellas to let them know I'm on my way.

"Hello," Ray answers on the other end.

"Ray, this Steve. You and Ted ready?"

"Just sitting here watching this game on cable waiting for you."

"Alright I'll be over in about 10 minutes. Be outside. Make sure you let Ted know. You know how you brothers are."

"Ooh look at that hit!"

"What happened?"

"The quarterback was just knocked out of the game. Good grief."

"Whatever. Just be outside when I get there. See ya in a sec."

"Bye."

What a nut. Ray would probably watch a football game before going on a date.

****

Those fools are actually outside waiting for me. That's a change. Ray and Ted. Those are my boys. Ray is about the most chilled out person I know. Cuz is so laid back that his reaction to being on fire would be to say, "Oh...I guess I should put this out." Only time I see this brother get excited is when he's about to go to the gym. Then again cuz is all cock diesel. Ted on the other hand would never set foot in a gym. Ted is more on the lean side. He keeps in shape by eating so sporadically and cracking jokes about people. "Alright, don't just stand there. Get in the car."

"I got the front seat," Ray says as he holds the seat so Ted can get in the back.

Ted smirks as he climbs in the back seat. "Forget you."

Ray gets comfortable in the front seat. "Where's this party anyway? Are the women going to be up in there or what?"

"Up in what? You sound like you expect to find women stuffed into a closet," Ted says, ever the comedian.

"They should be," I answer. "This attorney on my job is having the party."

"I can see it now. Bunch of people standing around eating finger sandwiches talking about some tough lawsuit," Ted says.

I shake my head. "Naw it won't be like that. Joe's cool. He just got out of law school. He's been at the firm for a few months. He's one of the few Black attorneys working there."

"So when are you going to law school?" Ray asks in his usual laid-back manner.

"Never. I see enough of what's going on to not want to be an attorney."

"Maybe, but you should really consider going to some type of grad school. You're too smart not to get another degree."

"Hey everybody can't be like you getting that MBA."

"MBA?" Ted cut in. "Isn't that the Mandingo Basketball Association?"

Ray looks back. "Ha ha, very funny Ted."

"Anyway," I say. "Let's talk about something else. I've been working hard all this week. Now I'm ready to party."

"All right then but you know I'm not going to let this drop Steve," Ray says as he leans back in his seat.

"Yeah Ray I know. You know cuz, you're a trip."

"Ray's more like a voyage," Ted adds.

"I mean it though," I continue. "One minute you're sitting back watching a football game or looking through somebody's swimsuit issue and then boom you're talking about the secret to life. What kills me is that your emotion doesn't change from one moment to the next. You're too cool."

"Just chilling."

I wish he would just chill and leave me alone about going to law school. I'm doing fine.

****

The party is kicking. The women are up in here and it's still early. Ted heads straight for the food. When he does eat he eats! Ray came in and some honies started checking him out. Some brothers have all the luck. Me, I try to be cool. I spot Joe chilling with a group of people. He sees me and immediately comes over.

13

"What's up Steve," Joe says as he walks up and grabs my hand. "Big daddy in the house!"

"Yo Joe, you weren't kidding when you said that you gave kicking parties. I'm having a good time and I've only been here five minutes."

"That's cool. Didn't you say that you were going to bring a couple of your boys with you?"

"Yeah, that's Ted over there standing by the chicken wings and Ray's over there...next to that fine young lady! Who's that?"

"That's Betty. She's the friend of a friend."

"Man I would sure like to be her friend."

"Calm down Steve. Didn't I tell you that you would like the party? Can I bring them in or what?"

"Yeah Joe, you're definitely a man of your word."

"So mingle, enjoy yourself. I have to get over here and talk to this young lady who's looking very lonely."

Joe walks away. He has to be one of the coolest brothers I know. Cuz is doing his thing as a young attorney who's on a mission. A serious ladies' man too. Women must like him because he's light-skinned. Then again Ray's dark-skinned and women fall all over him. I'm somewhere in between and have to work for all the play I get.

I don't know if I'm enjoying myself at this party anymore. I've been here an hour and no play. I might have to give Jo a call. Now that's a depressing thought. Other than a conversation here or there about sports, I haven't really talked to anybody. I asked a couple of women to dance. Of course they told me no. Wouldn't be so bad if I didn't see them dance with somebody right after they turned me down. Women are a trip like that. Hold-up, who's that coming in? Man she's fine. Jo might not be hearing from me tonight.

"Excuse me," I say as I approach the young lady. "Would you like to dance?"

She smiles. "I just got here but why not?"

"Right this way." I lead her past a group of people out to the middle of the floor.

We dance through four or five songs if you can call them that. It's mostly house music. It all sounds alike to me. I'm getting tired.

"Would you like to sit down for a minute?" I ask my dance partner.

"Sure, why not?"

I lead her to an open couch in another part of Joe's townhouse. I ask her name as we sit down.

"I'm Tamara, Tamara Johnson."

"Steve, Steve Walters." I extend my hand which she takes. "So Tamara, are you enjoying yourself?"

"Have to say that I am."

"Glad to hear that." Tamara is so fine! The sister has an even light-brown complexion, neck-length hair, and a beautiful face. One thing that strikes me about her is that she speaks in such a...an authoritative manner. Like she's used to being in charge.

"Do you know Joseph?" She asks, looking directly into my eyes.

"He works at my firm."

"Are you an attorney?"

"I'm a paralegal. I leave the hard stuff for Joe." Is it my imagination or did her smile fade slightly?

"Paralegal...that's good. How do you like your job?"

"It's alright."

"How long have you been there?" Tamara seems like she's interviewing me.

"I've been there for five years. Ever since I graduated from college."

"You have been a paralegal all that time?"

"Sure have. It's tough sometimes and sometimes it's fun depending on what they have me doing." She definitely looks like she's losing interest. "So what do you do?"

"I am an accountant with Brooks and McClure. I have been there for two years since I became a C.P.A."

"Wow you must really get paid."

"The money keeps the bills paid, however, I will not be satisfied until I am making millions running my own firm."

"You're certainly ambitious."

"We all should be."

"I guess so." Something about how she said that. I need to change the subject. "So what do you like to do for fun?"

"I like going to house parties. Usually given by somebody I know. I hate going to clubs. Most of the people in there are perpetrating anyway. I like going to cultural events like plays and music recitals. Sometimes I like sitting around my condo and listening to some jazz. Every now and then I like to go to the movies. I love going to dinner at fancy restaurants. What about yourself? What do you like to do for relaxation?"

My life isn't as active as hers. "I like parties, movies, just hanging out."

"Really?"

This is pushing it because she doesn't look like she's interested. "I would like to get to know you better. What's your phone number? Maybe we can take in a dinner and a play."

She smiles. Who would have thought? "Do you have a piece of paper?"

"Wait a minute." I reach into my back pocket to get out my wallet and pull out a business card. "Just write it here."

Tamara writes down her number. "All right, here you are. Maybe we can do something next weekend, movie and then maybe some coffee somewhere."

"That sounds cool." Man she's taking charge of the situation. I should ask her if she's going to pay. "Hey, they're playing a slow song. Would you like to dance?"

"I would love to," Tamara says as we stand up and walk to the dance floor.

Man she can slow dance. I can definitely get used to her.

****

"Steve, who was that woman I saw you with at the party? She was fine," Ray says as I'm driving him and Ted back to their apartment building.

"Her name's Tamara."

Ted cut into the conversation. "That girl? She looks high maintenance. You better make sure all your credit cards are paid up. The way she came in there I was expecting to see a tiara. I'm surprised she talked to you. Tell the truth. She made you bring her a drink and then she tipped you."

"Dag Ted. Maybe I just have it like that," I respond.

"You? You strike out more than...more than...now that I think about it, I don't know anybody who strikes out more than you do."

"That's cruel Ted," Ray says. "She was fine though. I didn't think you had it in you."

"Everybody else has supportive friends." I shake my head. "I'm going to give her a call sometime this week. We're already supposed to go to the movies next weekend. In fact it was more her idea."

"Bring lots of money Steve."

"She can't be that bad Ted."

"You better listen to him," Ray says. "This brother can probably tell you the color of a lady's underwear."

"Whatever," I grin.

We arrive at the fellas' apartment building. I ask them to get out of my car in my usual dignified manner.

"Get your bama asses out of my car."

"You need to work on your material," Ray says as they get out of the car. "Later Steve."

"Give us a holler next week," Ted says. "Oh yeah, all that stuff I said while in the car."

"Yeah?"

"I meant every word of it."

I watch those knuckleheads walk into their building and then I drive off. Man, Tamara has me all hot and bothered. I know the remedy. Let me grab my car phone. Punch in the right numbers.

"Hello," Jo answers in a sleepy voice.

"Jo, this Steve. Can I come by?"

"Steve it's three in the morning. Call me tomorrow."

"But I really need to see you tonight."

"You should have thought about that earlier. Now you want of make that booty call."

"Fine, I'll talk to you later."

"No...wait. Come on over."

"Talk to you in a few minutes." It's always good to have a standby.

Twenty-Three

Oh man. Where am I? Oh yeah that's right, I'm lying in Jo's bedroom. Can't believe I just didn't leave after we had sex. Then again I'm tired. I can't believe I'm still messing with Jo. Then again I shouldn't lie to myself. The sex is good. Even though she wants more. Well I want more too. More women. Jo isn't that bad though. She's about five-five, thirty pounds overweight, light-skinned with the plainest roundest face that I've ever seen. She wouldn't be that bad to walk around with in public, except that she gives me the goodies without doing all that. She's always available which is good. I probably wouldn't mess with her otherwise. I remember when I met her. She was working at the cologne counter at some department store. I was looking to restock my collection, so I was looking at some stuff at her counter. She showed me a few items and started asking a lot of personal questions. What I did for a living and if I had a girlfriend? She even said that she liked big men. I guess so since she was so big. Well I guess not that big but I like women built like swimsuit models. I remember I gave her my phone number and she called me up that night. Not that she had much to talk about. She seemed to be so impressed that I graduated college and was working at a law firm. She certainly was easy to impress since we had sex for the first time like a week later. She virtually threw herself at me. Now I'm laying up in her bed on this fine Sunday morning. I need to get out of here. Hmmm, I smell something cooking. Hey maybe she's hooking me up with breakfast. "Hey Jo! What'cha cooking?"

"I'm making some sausage and eggs for you. You want some toast and orange juice to go along with that."

"Yeah that'll be nice. Hook me up."

"Coming right up babe."

"Don't call me babe." I hate when she does that.

Breakfast wasn't bad. Ol' girl can cook. Probably make somebody a good wife. After I'm through with her of course.

"So did you like the breakfast?" Jo's smiling like a little housewife wannabe.

"I gotta give it to you. You can cook your butt off."

"I can cook a lot more for you if you let me. I can do a lot of things for you."

"I wish you would stop that mess. Everything is fine the way it is now."

"For you it is. What about me? I do everything you ask. I'm always home for you. I always do this stuff for you and you treat me like a kept woman."

"Kept woman? You learn that during one of your night courses."

"Are you trying to make fun of my classes?"

"You're too sensitive. I'm just having fun with you. What are you studying for anyway?"

"What do you mean by that? I told you that I want to be a social worker. I've told you that so many times. That proves that you don't listen to anything I say."

"Yeah, well, whatever." I really pay little attention to anything she says. Since this was a pretty good breakfast though, I'll show some interest. I hope it doesn't fire her up too much. "So why do you want to be a social worker?"

"I've told you that a thousand times too. I want to be able to help poor families. Homeless people. The downtrodden in this society."

She sounds like some of the radicals that I used to go to college with. The one's working in corporate America now. "Those poor families and homeless don't need any help. They need to get off of their asses and do something. I went to college and made something of myself. I'm getting paid."

"That's good what you did babe. I'm very proud of you. Everybody out there isn't like you. My father taught me that we have to help those less fortunate, especially if you've been blessed with something."

"Your father? The seldom-employed alcoholic? Isn't he using food stamps?" Oooh, I shouldn't have went there.

"Leave my father alone! He wasn't perfect. My family wasn't perfect but they did the best with what they had. I can't believe you said that! Why are you so mean?" Jo looks sad.

"Look I'm sorry. I shouldn't have said that. I meant what I said though about poor and homeless people. If they just get jobs, or study or do something they wouldn't be in the condition that they're in."

"You think it's just that simple don't you?" Jo was serious. "Don't you think that if most people had the opportunity they would go to school? Most people want jobs. Some people are not as fortunate as others. Sometimes people need a helping hand. We're all here to help each other."

"Forget helping others. I got mine. Let everybody else get theirs as long as they don't take it from me."

Jo looks disgusted with me. "It's too bad you have that attitude. I don't know why I deal with you."

"Hey don't act like this Jo." I walk around to her side of the dining room table and pull her to her feet.

"Don't try to sweet talk me." Jo smiles. She wants me to sweet talk her.

"You don't need to be stressing. Why don't we go work this out in the bedroom?" I lead her to the bedroom. A half-hour later everything is cool again.

****

I get home about noon. I immediately shower and change clothes. Then I sit down to watch a football game. The Eagles are

23

playing tomorrow night so I watch the Cardinals play the Giants. Of course like I do for every football game that doesn't involve the Eagles I fall asleep.

It's about eight now. Musta been really tired. I need to get something to eat. Then again I need to make a phone call to that nice young lady I met last night. Ted would probably say that I shouldn't call her right away. Then again Jessica once told me that women sit around wishing someone would call them. Whatever the case I've had Tamara on my mind since meeting her. Let me get the phone here. Get out her number. She has pretty hand writing. Let's see uhn, uhn, uhn, uhn, uhn, uhn, uhn. Here we go. One ring, two rings, three. Uh-oh, I'm about to get an answering machine. Waitaminute someone's picking up.

"Hello."

I try to sound as suave as possible. "May I speak to Tamara?"

"Speaking. Who is this?"

"Steve."

"Steve? Steve? Oh yes the gentleman I met last night. I am surprised you called so soon."

"I hate to waste time. I meant it when I said that I wanted to get to know you better."

"I see. I like it when a man shows some initiative."

Alright I made the right move. "That's me, Mr. Initiative. I'll go a step further. How would like to go see this play Saturday night. I know you said something about a movie and dinner but I have a better idea. We go out to dinner and then we go see that new play in town at Constitution Hall, The *Perfect Man.* It's been getting rave reviews."

"Sounds like a plan. I really do love a man with initiative. Really turns me on."

Yesss! "Glad to be of service."

"So tell me more about yourself. You said that you have been working at the same firm for about five years now. You must have received a lot of promotions."

"Not really. I get raises every so often but that's with everybody at the firm."

"So where do you see yourself five years from now?"

This is starting to sound like an interview. Maybe this is how she is. "I'll probably still be at the firm. My salary will probably increase and the benefits are great. They actually allow us to dress casually most of the time. It's rare that I wear a necktie to work. I don't have what you call a public contact position. Which of course suits me just fine. Plus even though they can work us hard sometimes, we have a good time around the office. I might retire from there."

"I see," she responds. Her tone of voice that suggests that she's disappointed. Then again it could be my imagination. "So what do you expect to be doing five years from now?"

"As I told you last night I expect to be running my own firm. Unlike some people I cannot see myself working for somebody else for the rest of my life. I have to have my own business. I will have my own business."

Man she sounds determined. "I like that attitude."

"You should," Tamara says in a matter of fact tone. "Steve dear, I have to get off the phone now. I have not worked out all day. Do you belong to a gym?"

"No." Is she trying to crack about my weight?

"That is too bad. Give me a call later this week. Talk to you soon."

"Yeah talk to you later." I don't know. I get mixed signals from this one.

Twenty-Two

Wednesday, hump day. This week at work wasn't as bad as last week. Things are kinda cool this week. We're just doing the regular copying and research. Nothing special. Me and the other paralegals spend most of the time in our little office talking about what guys usually talk about. Sports and women. Just me, Larry, and Hank. Larry's this big white boy. Listening to Larry is like listening to talk radio for recreational sports leagues. He's always telling us about what he did on the football field or on the basketball court. He's always trying to get me to come out to play football. I told him I wouldn't come unless I could play wide receiver. Larry's always telling me that his team needs linemen as if to say that since I'm so big I should be playing line. I haven't found time to make it out to a game. Maybe I'll play basketball with his team this winter. I'm probably a better football player than I am a basketball player so I'll go out there and just get the rebound.

Then there's Hank. Hank is a brother who is a serious dog. Cuz gets more phone calls during the day than some attorneys. Always a different woman. All of them seem to believe what he calls, "the requisite lie." Hank explained that the requisite lie is what men tell women who can't handle the truth. For example, Hank explained that if you have a young lady over at your apartment and the phone rings, when you pick it up it's probably your girlfriend. You have to tell your girlfriend that you're taking care of some business and the girl in your apartment that's hearing this conversation that the caller is a girl who you have no interest in who insists on calling. The requisite lie. Listening to these two makes the day go by.

Today everything is going by quickly. I did some research this morning for one of the associates. After that there was nothing left to do except sit around and chill. Chilling with Larry and Hank is always an adventure.

Larry is sitting at his desk, talking while he's playing a game of solitaire on his computer. "I'm fired up for my game this Saturday."

"What's your record now?"

"We're four and oh. Headed for a showdown Saturday with the team that beat us in the championship last year."

"You ready to play or what?"

"Born ready my man. I'm getting five sacks on Saturday."

"Dag Larry, you try to kill the quarterback don't you?"

"My girl Susie is always at the games. If you're going to have a bad game do it when your girlfriend isn't there."

"I hear you."

"Steve you should come out for the game. We can always use more linemen. I'm playing both ways now and special teams."

"Larry man, I don't see how you have the energy as big as you are," I laugh.

"I know you're not talking, tight as your pants been around here lately. Wait let me guess. The only exercise you get is lifting the fork to your mouth."

"I can't be the BIG time jock you are."

"That's right! I am big, beautiful, corn-fed, country boy out to kick some ass on Saturday."

"Well good luck."

"We'll have better luck if you come out on Saturday."

"Can't do that. I'll break a sweat. Then what will the ladies think about me?"

"Your big ass ain't getting no play," Hank says as he enters the room.

"I gets mine," I respond as I watch Hank take a seat at his desk with a stack of papers he has to go through.

"Yeah right. Your sex life is you and you."

Larry grins. "He got you my brotha."

"So what's up Hank? Who are you telling the requisite lie to tonight?" I'm thinking this should be good.

"Ummm." Hank looks like he's in deep thought. "I think I'll call Daphne tonight. I haven't talked to her in like a month."

"Isn't that the one you said had an ugly face but a great body?" I ask.

"One and the same."

"Hank my man. Why do you like messing with ugly women?" Larry asks.

"Yes tell us oh great master player," I say. I think that Hank is indeed a great master player.

"Well gather around children and I'll explain some of Hank Wilson's pickup principles. Soon to be coming to a bookstore near you." Hank sounds like a teacher. "First why waste time with a good-looking woman. A good-looking woman knows she has it going on. A good-looking woman knows that men will fall all over themselves to take her out. She can pick and choose at her leisure.

"An ugly woman on the other hand is not going to have that many men falling all over her. The exception being if she has a nice body. Now pay attention students, here's where it gets good. If she has a nice body, men will go after her because they think that they can easily get some. Of course these women may be ugly but they're not stupid. They know when somebody is trying to play them."

"But not smart enough to know when you're trying to play them," I comment.

"Quiet grasshopper before I body slam your fat ass," Hank says. "Anyways I see an ugly woman and approach her like she has some sense and like she's beautiful. I act like I'm interested in her personality. They eat this up so much that they just hand me the punanny. In most cases I don't have to ask. So remember, just be nice to them and tell them the what, students?"

"The requisite lie," Larry and I say on cue.

"Very good children. Now if you don't mind I need to get this work done since I've been on the phone all day.

****

It's near the end of the day when Joe comes in our office looking solemn. Something must be up since he closes the door behind him.

"Fellas," Joe says. "I want y'all to keep this under your hat."

"What up man?" Hank asks.

"Well," Joe responds. "I've been hearing on the grapevine that the firm is about to reduce some staff. Business hasn't been as good lately."

"Do you know who's about to be let go, Joe?" I ask.

"I'm not really sure, however, I've heard that it'll mainly be support staff, maybe some of the associates including myself, maybe even some of the partners."

"Some of the partners? Now I know it's rough," Larry says.

Hank holds his hand up. "But holdup Joe. They're thinking about letting you go? All the hard work you're doing around here."

"A lot of times these things are about politics," Joe points out. "Sometimes you can be on a job for ten years and work your butt off and still get laid off. Then somebody who has been on for a few months stays because he's buddy-buddy with the supervisor."

"I don't know Joe," I say. "I've been here for five years. Worked my butt off. Most of the time anyway. They must like me. I think I'll survive the layoffs."

Larry looks worried. "I hope I survive. I've been here two years and I'm just now starting to get on my feet. Thinking about marrying Susie, getting a house, starting a family. I hate to have to start all over again."

"You?" Hank shakes his head. "I'm trying to get an apartment. Living in my mom's basement ain't cutting it. I can't afford to lose this job."

"What about you?" I ask Joe.

"Well you know how it is," Joe says more to me and Hank than Larry. "Sometimes other people get jealous of you. Don't want to see you succeed."

"You seriously think they'll let you go?"

"The handwritings on the wall, Steve. You know what though, if they let me go I'll just start my own business where I can run things. Now how does that sound?"

"Sounds great man," Hank says. "If you need a paralegal just give me a call."

"Why don't we wait and see what's going to happen," I say calmly.

"Yes, let's all wait and see," Joe says distantly.

****

What a day at work. Everybody stressing because they're worried about being laid-off. I'm not worried. I've been there five years. They pay me a lot for a paralegal. I must be valuable to them. I work hard. Do everything they ask me to do. I may goof off every now and then but that's no more than anybody else. My job's safe. Larry will probably be there. The partners will even shoot the breeze with him. So both of us will be there. I don't know about Hank. Cuz will goof off too much. Always on the phone and wearing clothes like that purple suit he had on a couple of weeks ago. Hank needs to polish up his resume. He'll be using it soon. On the other hand I can't see how they would let Joe go. Maybe "other people" are jealous of him. Joe cracks me up. As light as he is, he's probably the most sensitive when it comes to matters of race. He needs to let that race stuff go. The only color that matters in this world is green. Which I will have plenty of for the rest of my life. I know my job is safe. Right now I need to give Tamara a call to finalize plans for our date. Man I can't wait to tear her up.

Twenty-One

Tamara lives way out here? White Oak, Maryland. I've been waiting to see her all week. Tonight's the night. I have my Italian suit on. Looking good. I need to think about losing weight. Suit's feeling kinda tight on me. I need to go on a diet. Better yet I should just buy bigger clothes. I'll stop by a store next week. Get me a nice wool suit since winter is coming up. Right now though I need to concentrate on Tamara. Man she has a nice body. Probably take me two days to enact all my fantasies about her. Then another three days to make up some more. Almost there. She wanted me to call her from the car to let her know when I'm close, so she can meet me outside. No problem there. Let me dial real quick.

Tamara picks up. "Hello."

"Tamara it's Steve. I'll be there in about five minutes."

"Okay Steve I will be outside waiting for you."

"Alright Tamara." This is going to be good.

I pull into the driveway of Tamara's complex. Then I see something that makes my heart jump. She is definitely made to perfection. Tamara has on a red evening dress that leaves nothing to the imagination. How that song go? Baby got back! Plus she has on some black pumps that are bringing tears to my eyes. I think I'm in love. I drive the car over to where she is standing. I put the car in park and walk over to her side of the car in order to let her in. She is so fine I'll make love to her right on the spot. She's so fine I'll make love to her shadow. "You look beautiful."

"Thank you Steve. You look...handsome yourself."

She sounded like she wanted to say something else. No I can't think like that. Let me just have a good time tonight. I get into the car and immediately put on a local top 40 station. The way her head is bobbing I guess Tamara enjoys the music. I try to keep my attention on the road. "So are you ready to see this play?"

"I certainly am ready. One of my girlfriends has seen the play already. She fell in love with the lead character. In fact she wants to see the play again."

"That's good."

"I am starved. Where are we going for dinner?"

"We're going to dinner at Marco's in Georgetown."

"Marco's. I'm impressed."

Alright! Scoring some points. "This brother named Dexter Williams has an ownership interest in the place."

"The CEO of DEX Enterprises. He owns a lot of property in the area. Marco's is a very expensive place. You sure that you can afford the prices?"

"No problem. I think I can handle it," I say with a confidence.

"Glad to hear that."

****

"The food here is excellent. I have to send my compliments to the chef," Tamara says as she's eating a chicken dinner that anywhere else would have cost $4.95.

"Yeah, I love coming here." The requisite lie. Only time I've been here is when my supervisor treated the paralegals to lunch.

"That surprises me. You really do not seem to like the type who would eat in this place."

The hell is she supposed to mean by that? "Why do you say that?"

"Marco's is a place for more...upscale people. Business owners, professionals, people like that."

"You're saying that I'm not a professional?"

"I did not mean to offend you. It is just that a paralegal is not considered a professional."

I keep my cool. "Maybe, maybe not. The term professional is kinda subjective anyway. Look, I get paid. More than a lot of professionals in this town."

"I guess you are right," Tamara says in way that sends chills up my spine.

"I guess you would qualify as a professional."

"College degree and master's degree. C.P.A. You are right, I qualify as a professional."

Man she sounded conceited when she said that. "Even though I don't know anything about your work you definitely seem competent. Do you supervise anybody?"

"I supervise five people. In another year I expect to be running a whole department."

"Like I said before you're definitely ambitious."

"Yes, ambitious."

Oh man she's giving me that look. "All that work, I know you're ready to have a good time."

"Oh yes," Tamara says real seductively.

Yeah baby I'm gonna get mine tonight.

****

After dinner and desert we leave Marco's to go see *The Perfect Man* at Constitution Hall. It's pretty good I guess. It's about this brother involved in relationships with two women. Each woman sees him as the perfect man. What a stupid story. Who buys that? I'm only paying so much attention to the play anyway. Tamara on the other hand is enjoying it. I'm enjoying how her legs are rubbing up against me and how she is leaning into me. Damn my joint is hard.

After the show I drive her home and she invites me to her condo. Oh yeah here we go. She tells me to have a seat and asks if I want anything to drink. I want to say a forty but don't want to appear tacky. I tell her red wine is alright. She goes into the kitchen to get to wine glasses and a bottle of red wine. When she returns she sits the wine glasses on the table and picks up the remote control to turn on her CD player. She put a Sade CD on. It sounds nice. It's a nice mood. Lights are dim. I uncork the wine bottle. We make a toast to ambition. We stand up and start slow dancing. I mean SLOW dancing. I shouldn't even say dancing. We're GRINDING. Oh man I'm going to tear this girl up! As we grind our lips start to touch. We start tongue kissing like long lost lovers. We're going for it. Man I thought I was hard before. I'm even harder now. I'm going to get some tonight! I start rubbing on her back gradually going down to her butt. Oh man does it feel nice. The same time she's rubbing on my back eventually going down to my butt. Dag, she's really grabbing me. I start lifting her dress slowly. Now she's putting on the brakes.

"Steve, that is far enough. We have not reached that point yet."

"Come on baby we were in a groove. Why stop it now?"

Tamara pulls away from me and sit down on the couch. "Steve I really think we should get to know each other better. There is just too much stuff out there to mess around."

"I guess you're right." I join Tamara on the couch. "I guess we really should get to know each other better."

"I just want to be sure. I have met too many jerks out here to mess around. "

"I can respect that." The requisite lie.

"Tell you what Steve. Just hold me. I feel good in your arms."

"I guess I can do that for you." I pull her towards me. We sit there just relaxing. Chilling to Sade.

****

I leave Tamara's about an hour later. She gave me one helluva good night kiss. She definitely gives me something to look forward to. Unfortunately I still have a killer hard-on. I know how to take care of it. Every time I go to this girl's apartment I worry if somebody is going to steal my car. I always say I'm going to leave this girl alone. Never quite works out that way. I arrive at her complex, park my car, and walk to her apartment. I called ahead, of course. I wanted her to be ready as soon as I arrived. I knock on the door.

"Who is it?"

"You know who it is."

She opens the door.

"Hi Jo. I'm feeling horny tonight."

"What happened Steve? That woman you went out with tonight didn't give you any."

"I didn't go out with any woman tonight. My firm had a function."

"Why didn't you tell me?"

"Do I tell you everything I do?"

"No but I wish you'd..."

I grab Jo, kiss her, and take her to the bedroom. Jo probably had the best time of her life. She didn't know that I was thinking about Tamara the whole time.

Twenty

I'm laid off! I'm unemployed. How could this happen!?! All week things were good. I made it all the way to Friday. I knew I had a job. Then this afternoon my supervisor Shellie started calling people into her office. I was cool about it. I saw a couple of people, some clerks, and a couple of the newer paralegals go into her office and then come out a little while later with sad looks on their faces. Suckers was all I could think at the time.

Until I was called into Shellie's office.

She told me some bull about my service being appreciated. How I was such a hard worker but how they couldn't afford me at my salary. You believe this! I get the boot and Larry and Hank get to stay. Hank! Brother spends all day on the phone. He wears party suits to work and I get laid off. What kinda world is this? Now I'm sitting here cleaning off my desk trying to make sense of all this. Larry and Hank are trying to console me. It's not really helping.

"That's real bad Steve. As hard as you work around here. I wish it didn't have to be this way," Hank says sincerely.

"Steve, my brotha. If there is anything that I can do for you let me know," Larry adds.

I try to sound optimistic. "You know what fellas, I'll just get another job. This is Washington, D.C. after all. All these law firms and attorneys. Somebody needs a paralegal. I'll probably be working next week."

"My man, I hope so," Larry says.

"You're a smart brother, Steve. You have experience. You'll probably get a job next week. You'll probably make more money. You know what I'm saying," Hank says.

"I know what you're saying Hank. Fellas I'll be back in a little while. Joe wanted me to stop by his office. See you later."

I walk into Joe's office while he's on the phone. I notice that he's been putting stuff into boxes. I guess he was unfortunate too. Though he doesn't look that way. He looks happy. He motions me to sit down. He hangs up the phone and begins to talk.

"Apparently you've been let go as well."

"Yeah Joe they gave me the boot."

"We could probably cry racism but more whites were let go."

Joe needs to let that racism go. "I'll simply get another job."

"That's the spirit Steve. I'm looking at this as a stepping stone. God has blessed me with what I have so far. I've learned a lot on this job. Saved up a lot of money too. This layoff is just the thing I need to get me into gear. I just got off the phone with this brother who's working as a solo practitioner. He was telling me that even though he's putting in long hours, the rewards of being your own boss are enormous. I couldn't let these white people boss me around forever. The only way for a brother to get ahead is to have his own business."

"I guess so." I never really thought about owning a business. Never thought past working for the firm.

"Steve you need to be more enthusiastic than that. You have to go out there and look for another job. The firm despite letting you go has promised to provide excellent references for everyone. Even you."

"Ha ha, Joe. I need to get my resume together. You know, I haven't looked at it in five years. I probably need to update it."

"Steve, you're not going to tell me that you haven't updated your resume. Man I can't believe that. In all your time here you haven't tried to find another job?"

"Nope. This job paid well, gave me great benefits. Provided me with a great sense of security. I seriously thought about retiring from here."

Joe shook his head. "Steve, you're an intelligent brother. Why are you wasting your life?"

"I'm not wasting my life. What do you mean by that?" I'm a little offended by the statement.

"I mean exactly what I said. Talking with you these past few months I realized that you are intelligent. Very intelligent. You should be getting a grad degree. Maybe even going to law school."

"I don't want to be a lawyer."

"You're intelligent enough to be whatever you want to be. You have talent. There's a passage in the Bible which basically says that if you're given a certain talent you have an obligation to use that talent for the good of others. You're supposed to multiply that talent."

"I don't think I'm all that."

"I'm sorry that you think like that. You'll wake up one day. Look, let's not end on a bad note. Keep in touch Steve and good luck finding a job," Joe says as he stands up extending his hand.

"You too Joe." I shake Joe's hand.

"I don't need luck. I have God."

****

Man what a day. Right now I'm chilling with Ray and Ted. Drinking a forty. I decided that I would party a bit before trying to find a new job. Maybe get unemployment. I have enough savings to pay rent and my car note for a little while. I'll worry about a job when the time comes. Right now I'm going to chill and watch this movie on cable. It's a good thing I have alcohol in me. This movie is terrible. Looks like it was made with a video cam.

"Yo Ray," I say between sips. "This movie is bad. Why are we watching it?"

"For laughs of course," Ray answers while sipping on a lite beer.

I'm starting to feel the effects of the alcohol in my system. "What's the name of this movie anyway?"

"It's called, *The Player Artist,*" Ray says.

"This movie should not have anything in the title suggesting art," Ted says. "I think I know how they made this movie. The producer and his boys were coming back from a real movie with some change left over from getting popcorn. The producer had this brain storm and told his boys to call up some of their skeezers. When they came over they drew straws to decide who would do what. The producer then got his mom's video cam because that's where the producer lived and started shooting."

I laugh my big ass off. "Holdup Ted. How did they manage to get it on cable?"

"Keep drinking your beer and listen," Ted answers. "After they finished the film they took it to a film festival where it came in last place in all categories."

"That still doesn't explain anything," Ray says between laughs.

"Just listen," Ted continues. "One of the actors in the film had a friend, whose second cousin knew the great-grandmother of a friend whose boyfriend had a sister whose girlfriend knew the secretary of the chief assistant to the vice president of the cable station for new projects. The secretary hooked everything up. Her name was Shaunita Meliqua Lanita Monifa Sherifah Betwina...Johnson."

Oh damn.

After the movie we sit around chilling. Me and Ray drinking some brews. Ted is talking to some girl on the phone. I like listening to Ted talk to women. He's the only man I know that can be totally honest with a woman and get away with it. At a party I heard him walk right up to a woman and say, "I think you're really attractive. I would really like to make love to you." She gave him her number. I try that and I get slapped.

"So Steve what are you going to do for yourself?" Ray asks, laid back as ever.

"Thought I'd just chill out for a little while."

"I mean with the rest of your life."

Oh no here we go again. "Ray, you're not going to jump on me about going to grad school are you?"

"Somebody has to do it."

"Everybody seems to be jumping on me about going to grad school. The brother who had the party we went to was telling me about going to grad school. Then I got you on my case every now and then. Even Tamara sneaks in little comments. As if she expects me to do more with my life."

"How is she by the way? You hit that?"

"Naw man. She says that she wants to get to know me better."

"You're not seeing the inside of them panties for a while then. You better stick with that skeezer over in Northeast."

"Jo? I'm surprised you remember me telling you about her."

"Don't get off the subject. You need to do something with your life. You seem like everything is cool but it's not. At the least you're going to have to get another job. At the most you need to do something to ensure your future. College degrees don't mean the same that they used to. To make it in today's world you need a college and grad degree."

"Ray man, a lot of people make it out there with nothing more than a high school diploma. If they can make it so can I."

"People getting far in life with just a high school diploma are few and far between. To make it you need to control your own destiny. The more education that you have the better are your chances."

"Whatever, I need to get out of here. I told Jo that I would come by tonight."

"You do this every time," Ray says in a serious tone of voice. "Every time we talk about something deeper than sports or women you run away. You find something else to do. You can't keep running."

"I'm not running. I'm just going to see Jo," I say as I stand up to leave.

"You are and the sad part is that you don't even realize it. I look at you and I see someone who letting his intelligence go to waste. You're wasting your life."

Wow Deja Vu.

****

"Hi what's up," I say as I step inside the door of Jo's apartment.

Jo hugs me. "Hey babe,"

"Don't call me babe."

"You want something to eat."

I sit down on Jo's living room couch. "No, I had something,"

"What's going on? You don't seem like your usual self tonight. What happened? Some girl told you no so you came over here to see me?"

"I was just laid off my job."

"Poor baby." Jo shows genuine concern as she reaches out to hug me. Her hug is surprisingly comfortable.

"Don't call me baby." I pull away from her. "It's no biggie. I'll just get another job."

"Getting laid off is tough. I got laid off a job one time. It sure didn't feel good. These things happen though."

"Yeah these things happen." I lean closer to Jo and kiss her. As always she responds immediately. I slowly lay her down on the couch as I reach down inside her pants to squeeze her butt. Ample as it was. I take my hand out to start unzipping her pants when she grabs my hand.

"Steve we can't do this tonight."

"What do you mean we can't do this tonight?" That's the last thing a brother with a forty of malt liquor in his system wants to hear.

"I mean we can't Steve."

I sit up on the couch. "Why not?"

"We just can't."

"Why are you tripping Jo?"

"My period's on Steve. Unless you're so horny you don't care. I'm just a little whore to you anyway ain't I?"

Well yeah. "If you told me that you had your period I wouldn't have come over tonight."

"That's the point Steve. You wouldn't have come over tonight. You would have stayed away. Despite how you treat me sometimes I really like being with you. I think you're smart and I think that you can go places but you know that. Sometimes though, I just don't know. I wonder why I even bother with you. You're not nice to me. You never take me out. I just don't know what I see in you."

"Maybe because I make you cum all the time. Maybe that's it. Whatever, you got your period. There's nothing we can do tonight. I'm outta here."

"Just like that? We can be intimate without you being inside me."

"Maybe but I don't feel like it tonight."

"Always running."

"What!?!"

"I said you're always running. Every time I confront you on something you're always ready to run away or change the subject. Why don't you stay and for once just sit over here and hold me, cuddle, watch cable with me. Why don't you just try that for once? Please."

"Look I'm gone. Bye." I walk to the door and open it to leave.

"That's right Steve run. Don't face anything. Waste your life by not standing and facing anything. Get out!" I've never seen Jo angry like this.

"Later for you then." I shut the door behind me.

49

Oh man what a day. I get fired, lectured to, and no booty to top it off. I'm just going to go home and chill.

Nineteen

I've been unemployed for about a week. Not that I'm complaining. All I did this past week was chill out, drink beer, go shopping, drink beer, watch the talk shows, and did I mention, drink beer. Ah the life. Watching the talk shows is a trip. One show had me dying. These five ugly women were on this one show complaining that they couldn't get a date because they were so beautiful. It must have been their inner beauty or there are several men in the world like Hank who play with the minds of these women. Man, I still can't believe they kept Hank on the job. I wonder how that knucklehead is doing. Larry too. Whatever. I need to get ready for my date tonight with Tamara. Man she cracks me up. She took the news of my getting fired pretty well. She saw it as an opportunity for me to do something more. Everybody's a trip. Everybody wants me to be more than what I am now. Doesn't anybody ever think that I might be content with my life now? Everybody wants so much. I just want to chill and enjoy life. Ah well. I need to get into the shower.

Man that shower felt good. Even though the bathroom scale didn't do anything for my ego. 245! I think I need to lose some weight. This is a long way from college. Back in college my weight used to stay around 180. I was a 180 pound six-footer. Yeah I was the man back then. Yeah right. Women paid less attention to me back then than they do now. I didn't know what was up. That's right I know. I was too much into books back then. I forgot how many times I made the Dean's List. Everybody thought that I was going to be somebody big. Didn't have much of a social life. Then there was...naw. Need to put her out of my mind. Things changed when I got out of school and started making money. It's funny, but back then I was seriously thinking about going to law school, but I started having too good a time outside of school to consider going back. Shoot, I make more money than most attorney's in this city anyway. Correct that, I made more money. I guess I should get another job in a couple of weeks. Did my resume. All I have to do is send it out and calls should start coming in. Time to get ready for my date.

****

Man, I can't believe a woman that's this fine is in my Baretta. Tamara had on this designer jacket and some jeans that even though they were loose showed her butt perfectly. I hope tonight's the night.

"So what are we going to see?" Tamara asks as we wait at a red light. The way she's looking into my eyes, she's ready!

"We're going to see *Predators Club*. It's a story about these four men who have a contest to see who can pick up the most women in a month."

"Sounds like something a man would enjoy."

Now what? "I read some reviews. The critics said women will love the movie."

"I'll take your word for it. Steve, how's your job search going?"

"I've been chilling this week. I did update my resume. I'll start sending out some copies next week."

"Good, good. You should go for higher paying position. Maybe even a managerial position."

"I'll send them out and see who calls."

"Do you have any type of plan? Any strategy?"

"Nope. But I'll be alright. I'll get something. I have too much experience not to get something good.

"Whatever you say." Tamara sounds disappointed. I swear I don't know about her sometimes.

****

The movie was pretty decent. Tamara enjoyed it more than I did. Tamara and all the women in the theater were going crazy over the men's bodies in the film. I have never seen anything quite like it. I mean Tamara looked like she was drooling over this one man in the film. Of course the way he was built he looked like a genetic engineering experiment. Made me feel self-conscious. The thing was how the women in the audience were going crazy. No wonder Ray spends so much time in the gym. No wonder he gets so much play. Then again, even though I'm not built like Ray I still get play. I'm sitting here in Tamara's apartment, sipping some red wine, listening to some jazz. Best of all I have Tamara snuggled up against me. Tonight's the night, I can feel it.

"So did you enjoy the movie?" I ask Tamara while rubbing her back.

"Oh yes. Ummmmmm," Tamara says as she snuggles on my chest. "Those men had some of the best bodies that I have ever seen. They can get a girl all hot and bothered any day."

"Checking out men's bodies like that. You should be ashamed of yourself,"

"Do not even try that Steve. Not the way you men buy the swimsuit issues that everybody's magazine seem to put out. I heard they even put out comic book swimsuit issues now. Women check out bodies too." Tamara squeezes my love handles.

I lift her head up and kiss her. Hard. Very hard. As we're kissing I lay her head back on the couch and reach under her shirt and start massaging her breasts. Man they feel good. This woman is perfectly proportioned. Tamara lifts my hands off of her so she could take off her shirt and bra. I go to work starting on her left breast while still massaging her right breast. After about twenty minutes I switch. I going to tear this girl up! Tamara stops and pulls my shirt over my head. Did she just frown? Must be my imagination. She motions me to lay on my back and then she starts licking my chest. Aw this feels good. Wait she's stopping.

54

Tamara sits up and puts on her bra and shirt. "Steve, this is going too fast,"

I thought it was going nice and slow. "What's wrong?"

"Steve, we have known each other a few weeks. There is too much stuff going around out there. We really need to wait."

Why me? "Okay, I can respect that," I try to sound sincere. "So now what?"

"I am going to have to ask you to leave. I have to get up for church tomorrow morning."

"No problem. I have to go to the bathroom real quick."

I wonder what happened. What could have made Tamara stop? Damn this bathroom mirror explains everything. I look pregnant. My chest looks like a woman's. My stomach looks disgusting. All this time I thought I was keeping everything tight. I've been lying to myself. I quickly put on my shirt, use the toilet, wash my hands, and head out to the living room to get my jacket. Tamara walks me to the door.

"I had a great time tonight Steve. Thanks for the evening," Tamara gives me a hard kiss.

"Talk to you later."

Man I can't believe I got this big. Maybe that's why Tamara wanted to stop. Then again she could see how big I was anyway. Maybe it was something else. She mentioned going to church in the morning. Maybe she's one of those religious types. No sex before marriage. Then again both Hank and Ted told me that those church going girls are sometimes among the freakiest, so I don't know. Maybe Tamara was actually turned off by my weight. Well I need to do something about that. I know just the person.

****

"So how do you like this gym so far," Ray says as we warm up on the stationary bikes.

"The women in here look good. I'm glad I came," I say between breaths. I'm really out of shape.

Ray effortlessly peddles on the bike. "Take your time Steve. You got to start off nice and slow. You don't want to overdo anything. You know what I mean?"

That thing with Tamara bothers me. I got the distinct feeling that she didn't want to go further last Saturday because of my weight. I can't miss out on a woman like that because of my weight. So I decided to join Ray's gym. I'm glad I did. They have everything in this gym. Free weights, indoor track, machines, and best of all, women. I thought Tamara was fine. The women here are fine. No wonder Ray is always at the gym.

After warming up for a little while, we go into the free weight room. Ray immediately grabs a curl bar and starts doing curls. Looked easy. He had 25 lb. plates on the bar.

"A little girl can lift that," I joke.

"Oh yeah? You try it."

"No problem." I walk over to where Ray put down the weight. I reach to pick it up. "Ugh." Damn it's heavy. I put it down immediately.

"I thought you said a little girl can lift this," Ray grins.

"A little girl on steroids. I'll try something else."

I walk over to the bench press and sit down on the bench. "How much is on here?"

"This is 135. You sure you want to start with this? You should probably start with a smaller weight."

"I'll be alright."

"You sure now."

"I'm sure."

"Okay. Let me get back there and spot you."

Alright all I have to do is lift it off the bench, bring it down to my chest and then lift it back up. Here I go. Man this is heavy! Weight feels like it's going to crush me. Oh good Ray's grabbing the weight and putting it back on its notch.

"You all right man?"

"Yeah Ray." It was heavier than I thought.

"You haven't lifted weights before have you?" asks this brother who comes out of nowhere.

"No, not really."

"When you're starting something new always start from zero."

"Got that right," Ray says. "Steve, this is Darryl. Darryl, Steve. Darryl's been around this gym for as long as I can remember."

"Yo what's up?" I ask as I extend my hand to Darryl which he takes.

"Not much bro. Joining a gym for the first time?"

"How can you tell?" There's something to Darryl. An aura or something. I don't a have a big brother, but there's something about him that suggests he would make a perfect big brother. I don't know what it is. Cuz definitely looks like he works out. His face is chiseled. Dark and chiseled. Cuz's eyes look like they're older than time. Cuz can't be much older than thirty. Something about him catches your attention.

"Someone coming into the gym for the first time will always bite off more than they can chew, especially a man. Will try to lift a big weight without having a foundation to do so. They end up not being able to lift the weight. They become frustrated. After joining the gym all gung ho they end up leaving after a couple of weeks. I've seen it a thousand times."

"Trust me Steve, if it's happened, Darryl's seen it," Ray remarks.

"Hush up now," Darryl responds. "Steve don't try to start at the top. All things have a beginning. That's where you should start. Start with the lowest weight in here and then gradually work your way up. Every house must have a strong foundation."

"Thanks man, I have to do that." Something about Darryl makes you want to believe every word he says.

"What are you trying to accomplish by coming to the gym Steve?" Darryl asks.

"I'm here to check out the women."

"Nothing wrong with that. There are some nice and intelligent young ladies that work out here. I hope, however, that you have a stronger motivation than that for paying this gym's membership fees."

"Straight up, I'm trying to lose some weight."

"Do you have a plan?"

"Not really. I thought I would come in here, ride the bikes, lift some weights. I figure the pounds will melt away."

"You need more than that bro. First you need to make a commitment to losing weight. That's first and foremost. Then you need a specific exercise program. You need a certain amount of aerobic activity. At least 90 minutes a week. That includes walking, running, swimming, anything that gets your heart rate up."

"Sex?"

"Actually studies have shown that one can burn calories during intercourse."

Ray smirks. "No wonder you're so big Steve."

I make a motion as if I'm going to back slap Ray.

"After the aerobics you have to make a commitment to lift two to three times a week. There must always be a balance." Darryl says.

"I see what you're saying," I say.

"Good. I need to get into my workout. I feel terrible if I don't get it in. Later brothers." Darryl turns and leaves the weight room.

"Darryl's the man," Ray says.

"Cuz must get a lot of play from the ladies."

"All the women here are friendly to him but he doesn't hit on anybody. I never really asked him, but I think he's devoted to one woman."

"Devoted to one woman? Now that's a concept."

"You crack me up talking like you're such a ladie's man. All you have is Jo who I don't think has good sense and Tamara who probably is not going to give you any."

"She's going to give me some. I'll call you while I'm doing it."

"You're nasty."

We laugh as we continue the workout. This time though I'm not picking up the big weight. This time I'm starting from zero.

****

I get home about 9:30. I'm feeling pretty good. I feel like I lost some weight already. I'll check out the scale in a few minutes. Need to make phone call first. She's picking up.

"Hello?"

"Tamara, this is Steve. What's going on with you tonight?"

"Oh hi...Steve." Tamara sounds surprised

"Tamara, guess what."

"What?"

"I joined a gym today. I'm going to try to lose some weight."

"Good for you. Nothing wrong with trying to keep your weight down."

"I also sent out some resumes today. I expect to hear something soon."

"That is very good Steve. Did you apply for managerial positions?"

"Naw, just regular paralegal positions at several firms."

"Oh." Now she sounds disappointed.

"We'll see what's going to happen." Man I can't figure this woman out.

"Steve dear, I have to get off the phone. I have something I need to take care of."

Did I hear someone knock on the door through the phone? "Okay no problem. You want to do something Saturday night?"

"We'll see Steve. I'll give you a call. Bye."

"Later."

Tamara's a trip. I'd probably leave her alone if she wasn't so fine. That was definitely somebody knocking on her door. This time of night? Maybe it was one of her girlfriends. Maybe it was some man.

Eighteen

I finally have a new job. After a month of being unemployed I finally have a job with this litigation support firm, Smith and Associates. It's just a temp job which is probably a good thing. I'm only getting paid by the hour. My hourly wage projected over the year represents a serious pay cut. No matter, I'll chill here until another job comes through. I haven't heard anything from any of the firms yet. I have hope though. This job doesn't seem that bad. Then again I've only been here for a couple of days. All I'm doing is summarizing depositions. Must have did this a thousand times at the firm. Sometimes I even trained other people on how to do it properly. One thing about this job is that I can come to work totally casual. Starting to get colder out being almost winter and all. So I'll probably wear sweatshirts and jeans to work.

The people I work with seem to be interesting. My supervisor is this white woman named Kathleen. She seems all right. I have about ten co-workers, all of us grouped into this one section of this big open floor. Most of the other space was taken up by people working on coding projects. Now that's something that looks like a moron can handle. I hope I don't sink that low. Of my co-workers, even though I've been introduced to all of them, I've been friendly to two of them. One of them is this brother named Dwayne. Cuz is very ordinary looking and quiet. He's maybe an inch taller than me, slim and wears big glasses. He seems to go about his work in a state of bliss. The thing that strikes me about cuz is that he's always reading the Bible. During breaks and lunch cuz is deep into the book. Amazes me, but then again I wouldn't consider myself the most religious person in the world. I'm not sure about God.

The other co-worker that I've been friendly to is Stephanie. Now she's fine. Finer than Tamara in my opinion. Ol' girl has high cheekbones, nice full lips, and an athletic body. Stephanie doesn't have a boyfriend, but from hearing her talk she's interested in some brother named Robert. This Robert is supposedly an executive with some bank in the area. Too bad because I would sure like to get to know her better, especially with Tamara and even Jo acting weird lately. Right now though I'm trying to get my hooks into Stephanie. "Stephanie, what going on for you this weekend?"

"Hanging out with my girlfriends. We're going to check out a couple of clubs. What about yourself?"

"I'll probably hang out with my boys." I hope to spend some time with Tamara or Jo. Maybe both. I don't tell Stephanie that. Hank always told me to avoid telling another woman about your female friends if you can help it.

Stephanie has a mock look of pity in her eyes. "You don't have that special lady to hang out with?"

"No I don't." The requisite lie.

"Don't worry, hang in there. You're a handsome man."

"Thanks. I'll keep that in mind. What about you? Still waiting for Robert?"

"See, I knew I shouldn't have mentioned him to you. You might go out and find somebody else and leave me all alone."

I know she's just flirting, but she doesn't know how fast I would jump on her if she ever got serious. "Now I wouldn't do that. You have my eternal devotion."

We laugh as we continue to summarize the depositions.

At break time everyone get up to stretch. Dwayne true to form pulls out his Bible and starts reading. Cuz cracks me up. He'll start reading for a minute and then start smiling as if he's read something amusing. "See something good Dwayne?"

"Whenever I read the Bible Steve, I always find some passage that's relevant to my life. It's amazing how when I'm feeling down and need some inspiration I can say a prayer and God will show me the answer in a Bible passage or even the statements of others. God has truly blessed me."

"That's good man." People like Dwayne crack me up. God this and God that. Always smiling and always upbeat. Like God's good to everybody. If God is so great why am I on this job instead of back at the firm where I belong? I decide to change the subject. "So Dwayne, when are you going to start studying for the bar?"

Dwayne had finished law school and he decided to wait for the February bar exam in Pennsylvania.

"I'll probably start studying in December."

"Do you think you'll be ready?"

"I will. I pray about it every day."

Again with the praying. "That's good. I need to go to the bathroom. I'll be back in a second."

"Okay," Dwayne smiles.

I get up to leave. "What's so funny?"

"You always walk away or change the subject when I talk about God."

"Do I? Never noticed."

"You do it all the time."

"I guess I'm not big on prayer or God.

"Well when God needs you he'll find you."

"Whatever." What did he mean by that?

****

I've only gone to the gym a few times since joining. Even when I do go I don't work out that hard. I'll lift a few weights and ride the bikes. I'll even do a couple of laps on the indoor track. Until I get tired that is. I can't understand how somebody can work out that hard. I'm still getting some results. I've lost a couple pounds since I started working out. Ted said that I lost weight because I can't afford food like I used to. Whatever. Money has been short. Bill collectors haven't started calling yet. Hopefully I'll have a real job before that happens. After all, I have to continue living the lifestyle to which I've grown accustomed. Anyway this workout stuff is for the birds. Ray must be a serious bird then because cuz is constantly going full tilt lifting the weights or doing the aerobic exercises. I don't know how he does it. I decide to ask him as I chill on one of the benches while he's doing curls. "Ray man. You work out like you're a professional athlete. What's up?"

"I do this to relieve stress. Between work and school, a brother can get stressed out."

"You? Stressed? As laid back as you are? Please. As hard as you work out you still look so cool doing it. You crack me up."

"Just chilling. You losing any weight Steve?"

"I've lost a couple of pounds."

"I can't really tell."

"Thanks for the support Ray."

"No problem. How's your new job?"

"It's alright. Something to do until I get a permanent job."

"How's the search going?"

"The resumes are out there, I'm just not hearing back from anybody. I guess they're taking their time before making a decision."

"I hope you hear something soon."

"I hope so too."

Ray changes the subject. "How're your ladies doing?"

"They're alright."

"Tamara give you any yet?"

"Damn Ray. All into my business."

"Don't front Steve."

"Naw man. She's always coming up some excuse. Always when we're about to get into something. I think she's trying to play me. I need to move on."

"Do whatever you have to do Steve. What about Jo?"

"Jo is just Jo. I don't know what to say about her. She'll always be there."

"If you say so."

"You sound skeptical."

"You can only dog a woman for so long. Women aren't as stupid as we like to think they are. If anything they think circles around most men. My dad used to tell me that women really ran the world. They just let men think we run the world because it's easier to let us think that way."

"You know Ray, I think you have a point."

****

I get home, shower, and get my clothes ready for work tomorrow. There's nothing on TV tonight so I decide to give Tamara a call. I haven't talked to her in a couple of days. I haven't seen her since last week. We were supposed to go out this past Saturday, but at the last minute she had an emergency and had to cancel our date. She never did tell me what the emergency was about. I dialed her number. "Tamara what's up?"

"Not much Steve. What are you doing?"

"Just lying on my couch relaxing. I got back from the gym a little while ago."

"How are your workouts going?"

"They're going along just fine."

"Are you losing any weight?"

"I've lost a couple of pounds."

"That is good."

"Did you resolve that emergency?"

"Emergency? What emerge...oh that emergency. Yes everything is fine. Thanks for asking. You're so sweet."

"You still owe me a date. How would like to check out this party that's going to be at this hotel on Saturday night?"

"Who's giving it?"

"A couple of brothers who apparently have money to burn. I heard their parties are always kicking. A lot of professional types will be there."

"Sounds good. Let us talk about it tomorrow. I have company over right now."

"Who's over there with you?"

"I am with a friend."

"Who's with you?"

"Do not get into my business. I will talk to you tomorrow. Good bye Steve."

"Bye Tamara." Dag she hung up the phone before I could get a word out of my mouth. I wonder if her friend is a guy.

Seventeen

I'm ready for the party at this big hotel downtown tonight. Got this nice suit that fits perfectly. I bought it at this men's shop. Specially tailored for a man of my size. Even though I've been going to the gym the weight has been coming off very slowly. Good thing I have this suit for my date tonight with Tamara. She said that she was going to wear this sexy short black evening dress. I can't wait to see her in it. I would rather see her out of it. I hope tonight's the night. Then again I always hope that. I don't know, but something's up with Tamara. She's been acting real funny lately. Canceling dates, not returning phone calls right away, having late night company. Late night company? Yeah right. Probably some brother. Tamara's been acting secretive about it all. I shouldn't worry about it unless something becomes too obvious.

After all she's going out with me tonight. That means that I'm the man. Yeah I'm the man. Time to get ready.

****

Tamara looked so fine when I picked her up. Sometimes I just can't believe that I'm with her. That black dress fit oh so well. Brings tears to my eyes. When we got to the hotel a lot of brothers were checking Tamara out. A lot of sisters were checking her out as well. I had always heard that women check each other out at parties and clubs. Mainly to see what each other is wearing. Yeah we make a good looking couple.

The party is kicking. Very crowded. A whole bunch of young Black professionals. People are exchanging business cards left and right. That's just in the lounge area. In the main ballroom people are jamming to the latest top 40 and house music. After me and Tamara have a drink we dance. Man she can move. It always amazes me how a woman can dance while wearing a tight dress and high heels. It amazes me more that they don't seem to break a sweat. I move a little a bit and break a sweat. After dancing through about four songs Tamara and I sit down.

"Do you like the party so far?" I ask Tamara as we sit down.

"It is very nice. A lot of people here." Tamara looks around the room. Her gaze lingers on different men. Damn.

"Tamara I know that I've told you already, you looks good. Good enough to eat."

"You wish," Tamara flirts.

"More than wish," I whisper in her ear. "We've been going out for a couple of months. A brother can only wait for so long. We need to take that big step tonight."

Tamara strokes my thigh. "You have a point there baby."

"Go up any higher and you might find a big surprise."

"Oh really," Tamara says seductively.

"Yes." Yes, something's going to happen tonight. I can feel it.

"Steve dear, hold tight, I need to go to the ladies room." Tamara gives me a kiss on the cheek.

I watch her walk to the ladies room. Man she's fine. Tonight is definitely the night. I can feel it. Man she's fine. She's so fine that she should go kiss her parents for such good work. Maybe she's so hot tonight because I lost a few pounds. I should really try to keep this weight. Man she's fine. I'm going to tear her up tonight. I wouldn't mind tearing up a couple of women here. There are some beautiful women in this ballroom. Maybe in a month after I get through with Tamara, I'll come to one of these parties and find a new woman. Yeah I'll do that. I figure once we have sex Tamara will be pressed about me the way Jo is, That way I can call Tamara when I need to make a booty call. Speaking of which here she comes now.

"That was quick," I mention as Tamara sits down.

"I wanted to make sure everything was still straight."

"Straight as ever."

"Thanks baby."

Baby! It's funny but I usually hate when a woman calls me baby. Really irks me. Except when Tamara says it. "Tamara, a slow jam is on. Let's dance."

I lead Tamara out to the dance floor. I can feel several people looking at us. Yeah I'm the man. We slow dance. Very sensuously. Oh man we are in rhythm. This feels too good. Oh man she's fine.

****

We arrive at Tamara's condo after having a great time at the party. As usual Tamara has a bottle of red wine waiting and jazz CD ready to go. The CD was something by Stanley Clarke. The music comes on and we slow dance. The same as we do all the time. We are in a groove. We kiss. Man she has soft lips. She feels so good. I start to pull her dress up. She stops me which shocks me because I believe that she would be ready tonight. This is driving me crazy. Tamara lets go of me and straightens her dress. "What's up?"

"What do you mean?"

"Every time we're about to get into it you put on the brakes. It's like you're trying to play me."

"Steve, sit down. We need to talk." Tamara sits down on the couch. While doing this she uses the remote control to turn down the sound on the CD player.

I sit down next to Tamara. "Okay what's up?"

"Steve the best way to say is to come right out. I do not want to sleep with you."

"Tonight?"

"Ever."

"What happened to bring this on?" I try to mask my hurt feelings.

"Steve you are a nice guy, but I have to think about the future. I do not mean to hurt you. Even though I have a good time with you I do not see you in my future."

"Why not? What are you trying to say?"

"Steve, I am an ambitious person."

I'm getting angry. "So are you saying that I'm not ambitious?"

"You do not seem like you are trying to get anywhere in life. You got to a certain point in your life and now you are content to stay there. Look at you. Working on some little temp job. Not trying to further your education. All fat and...sorry."

Damn. "So that's part of the problem?"

"I might as well be honest with you. I prefer men with more muscular and slim bodies."

"Why did you go out with me then?"

"Steve, I wanted to try to get past your weight, but in the end I cannot. I am sorry. It is not just your weight Steve. It is your attitude. You act like you do not have any ambition. I need a man who is going to go as high as I want to go. Someone with no ambition will just hold me back. I cannot allow that to happen. I was on welfare when I was a child. I know how it feels to go without."

"So?"

"You do not get it do you?"

"You're right, I don't get it. Look if you don't want to have sex I might as well just leave."

"Steve just because I do not want to have sex with you does not mean we still cannot be friends."

"Friends? Yeah right. I get to sit up here and listen to you talk about another man. Speaking of which, tell me the truth. Those times when you canceled a date or when you had late night company, it was a man wasn't it?"

"Yes it was. We have gone out a few times. We have not been intimate."

Like that makes me feel any better. "Let me guess. He's ambitious with a great body."

"He has what I want. Steve I am sorry it has to be this way."

"Yeah I'm sorry too," I grab my coat and let myself out of Tamara's condo. Forget her!

****

Sunday afternoon. I still can't believe that Tamara did what she did. Women! I'll never understand them. Led me on all this time. Then had the nerve to start seeing another man while going out with me. She was probably lying to me about not having sex with this man. Damn. It's a good thing I still have Jo. Jo's not that bad. I should go see her. In fact I'll go surprise her. She's always there for me. Maybe I should be nicer to her. Yeah, I'll surprise her.

****

I get to Jo's apartment and knock on her door. No answer. Maybe she isn't here. I knock again. I hear somebody coming now. Look like somebody's looking through the peephole. Ah the door's opening.

"Steve what are you doing here?" Jo looks very surprised while wearing a bathrobe.

I study the funny look on Jo's face. "Came to see you Jo,"

"Why didn't you call first? You usually call first."

"Well I didn't. Here I am though. You gonna let me in?"

"I can't do that right now."

"Why not?"

As if to answer my question a voice calls out, "Who dat at the door?"

"Just a friend," Jo responds back to the voice.

"Just a friend?" the voice questions. "Hold up, I'll be out there."

I look past Jo and see this big mean looking brother walking out.

"Yo who dis?"

"Just a friend Buster. Like I said," Jo says to this thug. "Don't worry about anything. Just go and chill out. My friend is leaving? Right Steve."

"Yeah I guess so." I turn and leave without looking back.

****

"This hasn't been your weekend has it Steve?" asks Ray. Ray, Ted, and I are watching the beginning of the Packers-Bears game on TV.

"Naw cuz it hasn't."

"Steve, who do you like in this game?" Ted asks.

"The Bears."

"I'm going with the Packers then. The way your luck is I wouldn't trust any of your picks."

"That's cold Ted," Ray says as he's munching on some potato chips.

I sip some beer. "Damn Ted don't you ever let up?"

"No. If you can't handle the heat stay out of the kitchen," Ted says while drinking a soda.

"So what you going to do now?" Ray asks.

"Heck if I know. Tamara gave me the boot and it looks like Jo did too."

"I tried to warn you about Tamara," Ted says. "I could see what she was about from a mile away. As for Jo...you can only dog a woman for so long before she gets tired of it."

"Yeah, but Jo was with this big thug looking brother."

"So, as long she likes him."

"Steve, you need to get over both of them," Ray says. "There's plenty of women out there. Here's what you should do. First start working out at the gym a little bit harder than you do. You start losing that weight and the women will claw all over you. Then apply to a grad school, get a degree, and then even more women will grab all over you."

"You just had to stick that grad school stuff in there didn't you?" I ask Ray.

"Somebody has to stay on you."

"Whatever."

"You need to do something."

"Like I said, whatever."

Sixteen

Pumping. Pumping. Yeah boy. I've been working harder these past two weeks since I last saw Tamara and Jo. I'm so mad. At Tamara for the way she did me and at Jo for being so disloyal. I haven't spoken to either one of them since then. I just go to work and to the gym. I've been getting more into exercise. I was shamming at first. Darryl gave me a good program to work out with. Darryl. I've never seen such charisma. Cuz gets much respect around the gym. He told me that he works as a counselor at a boy's home plus he's active in other areas. One thing that strikes me as interesting about the brother is that he says that he's a one-woman man. I normally wouldn't believe a brother who told me that but after meeting his girlfriend Sharon, I can see why. Fine as she was I'd stay loyal too. She was so cool when Darryl brought her to the gym last week. Cool and fine. I wish I could find a woman like that.

I'm starting to enjoy my workouts. I've lost eight pounds in the last couple of weeks. That isn't bad during the holiday season. Then again it isn't like I've been eating like crazy. I didn't eat that much during Thanksgiving. Could hardly get to the food. Everybody was over at my grandparents' place eating like there was no tomorrow. I was lucky to get a biscuit. It was good to get back up to Philly for the holiday. Seeing my parents and all. Even my little brother and sister. Little. My brother is bigger than me eating that college food and playing football. My parents did ask too many questions about my job status. My father was even all right to talk to. For once he seemed genuinely happy to see me. Pops is always on me about something.

Pumping. Pumping. Man I never thought that I would enjoy this. I usually start my workout by running around the indoor track. When I first started I could barely make one lap around the track. Now I can make four. Three more and I can make a mile. I'll get there soon. After running I hit the weights. I can now bench press 135. I can even get up to 165. Not bad. All the weights are getting easier. I'm starting to leave the gym with a good feeling about myself, especially since women are checking me out more. Man it's a good feeling. Funny thing is that I haven't tried to hit on any of them. I'm focusing on my workout. Then again that's what Darryl said that I needed to do. He said that when one focuses, the path becomes clearer. I definitely see what he's saying. Speaking of Darryl, there he is now.

"Yo Darryl, what's up cuz?" I yell while riding the exercise bike.

"How are you today sir?"

"Not bad."

"I see that you've been working out harder lately. Your girlfriend dumped you?"

"Naw, I'm tool cool for that." Darryl's amazing. I never told him about this thing with Tamara and Jo.

"Cut the bull. I've been around too long. You don't go from working out soft to working hard unless there's some motivation from anger. My guess is that it's a woman."

"You got me there. How did you know?"

"Bro, the first wars were fought over women. Think about Helen of Troy. No telling how many people died because somebody thought she was fine. Men have joined the French Foreign Legion because of women. Men have betrayed their country because of women. Men would lead peaceful lives if not for women."

"Sounds like you're hard on women."

"Not at all bro. That was just the negative side of women. The positive is that a woman, especially a strong woman, can lift a man up to the stars. Women, through their love possess a great power, the power of their love. The world would probably be better off if they ran the place."

"Ray told me that women really run the world. They just let men think we do because it's easier."

Darryl grins. "That statement isn't too far off the mark. In some cases they need to take more control."

"Ain't that the truth."

"You don't have to tell me about this woman or women as the case may be. Convert any anger that you may have into something positive."

"Thanks man."

"No problem bro. I have to leave now. The boss needs me for something tonight."

"You're working tonight?"

"Naw bro. My real boss, Sharon. I'll kick it with you later."

Twenty minutes later I finish my workout. I feel good.

****

Saturday night chilling with Ray and Ted. Never thought I would hang out with the fellas so much. I probably wouldn't if I had some woman to chill with. Then again it's kinda good to hang with the fellas. We usually talk about sports and women. Sports and women. A friend once told me that a man can go anywhere in the world and strike up a conversation if the subject is either sports or women. Tonight it's women.

"Women," I say after getting enough beer in my system. "What are they good for?"

"It's been too long for you if you have to ask that question," Ray laughs as all of us are watching some stupid movie on cable.

"Seriously though… Why do we really need them?"

"I'll take this one Ray," Ted says. "Women…they're God's cruel joke on men. If not for women we could sit around, drink beer, let our hair go nappy, not bathe, and fart in peace. Except for the cruel joke."

"What's the cruel joke?" I ask Ted. This dude is funny.

""By providing men with...Johnsons, God played a cruel joke on us. God provided men with this great appendage. Unfortunately it gets us into trouble because it draws us to women. For all the pleasure it can give us we need women in order to maximize the pleasure."

"Not all of us need women to maximize the pleasure," I say with a lisp.

"You and Ray notwithstanding, the normal among us need women. This causes us a lot of trouble. A man will work 60 hours a week to make a fistful of money. And you know what! Half that money, after Uncle Sam gets his cut, will go to supplement a women's income. All because of the cruel joke."

"You're a trip Ted," Ray laughs.

"Wait there's more," Ted continues. "The cruel joke will make a man cause bodily harm to himself. He will change his habits. He will take a woman to an expensive restaurant where he can't pronounce anything on the menu. Go to a woman's apartment. You find all sorts of examples of the cruel joke there. First of all a man who thought he might get some helped her move in, for free. Everything she has was bought by some man...because of the cruel joke. The best place to find an example of the cruel joke is at a wedding. Everybody is smiling except for the groom. The cruel joke has got him into this mess. In fact, it's the cruel joke that's keeping him from bolting."

"Dag Ted," I say.

"Holdup, the cruel joke is working in other ways at the wedding," Ted goes on. "The father of the bride is happy because the daughter's presence in the house was curtailing his sex life. The best evidence of the cruel joke at the wedding...the throwing of the garter. I went to this wedding one time. I swear this happened. This fine sister caught the bouquet. So when it came time to throw the garter, brothers were jockeying for position like it was the NBA. I'm not going to lie, I was in there too. She was fine! Anyway the groom threw the garter...all hell broke loose. The garter landed on the floor...everybody was diving for it."

"You too?" Ray asks.

"Darn right!" Ted yells. "The woman who caught the bouquet was so fine I wanted to give her my wallet. The brother who emerged from the pileup, and I do mean pileup, looked like he just scored the winning touchdown in the Super Bowl. All because of the cruel joke."

I'm laughing like crazy. "You're a trip."

"I try," Ted responds.

"That's why the women go crazy over him," Ray says to me. "He keeps them laughing."

Ted shrugs. "That's right, while they're laughing they don't seem to mind that I'm undressing them,"

"Fellas," I say. "New Year's Eve is just around the corner. Where's the party?"

"You might want to get through Christmas first," Ray points out.

"Gotta get an early start on these things."

"We'll let you know. This movie is stupid. Ted how did they make this movie?" Ray asks, giving Ted an opening.

"Well," Ted says. "They were just coming off of vacation from sunny Newark, New Jersey. They had a couple of blank video tapes left..."

Fifteen

A couple of days. A couple of days and it's the New Year. Work's been going alright. I'm sitting here kicking it with Dwayne and Stephanie. Dwayne is cool to talk to when he isn't talking religion. He's actually a big sports fan and player. I can't really see him playing sports, he seems so peaceful. Right now he's playing in a church basketball league. He's excited because his team won a big game last night. "Did you get off in the game last night Dwayne?"

"The Lord gave me strength for a great game last night. I scored 12 points. Passed well. Grabbed a couple of big boards."

"Afterwards you guys had a couple of beers right?"

"Steve you know this is a Christian league. After the game we said a prayer and then had fellowship with the other team. We're out there having a good time, celebrating what God has given us."

We need to get on another subject. "So Dwayne, what's going on for New Year's Eve?"

"My wife and I are going to church for midnight service."

Nice try Steve. "That's good Dwayne."

"You're invited to come out."

"Thanks Dwayne, but I'm going to a party with some of my friends."

"You're always welcome to come out Steve. The church doors are always open."

"I'll keep that in mind."

We chill out for a little while and then get back to summarizing the depositions. Well, everybody else starts doing that. I'm sitting here daydreaming. I've lost fifteen pounds since I started working out. I'm down to 230. I still have a ways to go. I've been daydreaming a lot lately. I guess because this job is boring. I keep imagining myself in a different job at some law firm making more money than I used to make. There has to be something better than this. Hmmmm, somebody say something.

"Steve, wake up," Stephanie says. "You looked like you were spaced out for a second there."

"I'm in my own little world Stephanie."

"So what are you going to do for New Year's Eve?"

"I'm going to this party with a couple of my boys."

"Now Steve, I thought it was going to be you and me alone in some big hotel suite."

I wish. "You wish. So what are you going to be doing?"

"I'll be hanging out with some of my girlfriends. There's going to be a big party at the *Pavillion*. Everybody who is anybody is going to be there."

"I'm not going to be there."

"Like I said everybody who is anybody is going to be there."

"Why you play me like that?"

Stephanie bats her eyelashes. "Only because I love you."

We go back and forth like this the rest of the day.

****

New Year's Eve. A chance to start over. I need a new start. The past couple of months have been kinda rough on me. Losing my job and all. Then again I was able to find something else even though I deserve better. Way better. It's good that I've lost some weight. When I went home for Christmas my family was gushing all over me, especially my mother. She was wondering if I was sick or something. Mothers are like that. Always worrying about you. Pops was his usual self. He asked if I was trying hard to find another well-paying job. Pops. I could be president of the United States and my father would want more. Yeah imagine that, a Black president. Anyway it's not like I can be a big time doctor like he is or a college professor like my mom. I wish they would let me be me.

Time to start getting ready for this party. My clothes are fitting way better. Man, these gray pants, I haven't been able to wear these in ages. Well I'll be able to wear them tonight. Ray said that there would be some fine women there. It would be nice to meet a new woman. I haven't had any for a while. I thought about calling Jo but decided against it. I still can't believe that she had another man in there. I can't believe that she would be that disloyal. Dag, look who's talking. I don't even know what to do about Tamara. I wish I tagged her before we split up. Man I...uh oh, the phone. "Yo."

"Yo? You think you're Rocky or what?" Ted says on the other end of the phone.

"What up fool?"

"The cracked plaster in this apartment. Fixing things on a timely basis isn't a concept to the owners of this building."

"Dag cuz, you got a comment about everything."

"Everything has a joke in it. People take themselves too seriously."

"Yeah I guess so."

"What time are you coming to get us?"

"In about an hour."

"Aw'ight. Call before ya come. See ya in a little while."

"Holla at you." I hang up the phone.

Time to get ready for the New Year.

****

I pick up Ray and Ted and drive down to Alexandria for the party. The party was at the townhouse of a friend of Ray's. It was a nice place. I wish I could afford a townhouse. I guess I would need another job first. I need to think about doing something. My lease is up next month. I don't know if I can afford to pay the rent on my place. I may need to get a smaller place. Smaller place. I already have a large one bedroom now. It still doesn't seem like I have enough room. Ah well, I'll worry about that later. The women are fine here. Even though they're not the ones I'm used to dealing with. These women are more ordinary. Less like Tamara and more like Jo. I'm having a good time because everybody here is so down to earth. Everybody is standing around eating or dancing. I'm chilling with some brothers talking about tomorrow's bowl games when Ray comes up with this attractive young lady.

"Steve I want you to meet a friend of mine. Darlene this is Steve. Steve, Darlene."

"Nice to meet you," Darlene smiles.

"The pleasure is all mine." Darlene's attractive in a plain sort of way. For one she's tall, about an inch or two shorter than me. She has light brown skin. She has a pretty nice body from what I can see through the blouse that she's wearing. Nice ass. She looks like she could stand to lose a couple of pounds. Just a couple though. She has a cute face. No makeup. That alone makes her look attractive. A lot of women would look better without makeup.

"Ray said that you are a paralegal," Darlene says enthusiastically.

"You've been telling her about me haven't you?" I ask Ray.

"So sue me. Look, y'all get to know each other." Ray walks away.

I turn to my new acquaintance. "So Darlene, are you enjoying the party?"

"It's all right. Yourself?"

"It's alright."

"So you know what I do for a living. What do you do?"

"I work as a temp. Mostly clerical."

"The job I'm on now is temporary."

"I know. Ray told me that you lost a job at this law firm."

I really need to talk to Ray. "Yeah it was tough but I'm surviving. The job I have now is holding me over until something else comes through."

"You seem like you can get a job anywhere you want."

I wish that were true. "I try my best."

"Ray said you graduated from St. James University in Philadelphia."

"Wow Ray must have given you my whole biography."

"Just the good stuff," Darlene laughs. She seems really pleasant. I feel comfortable around her.

"You want something to drink? Wine?"

"I'll take a beer."

"Beer? I thought you'd say something like red wine."

"I really don't like wine."

"Beer? A woman after my own heart. I'm a beer drinker myself. I'll be back in a second."

After getting the beer. Darlene and I start talking a bit more. She not only drinks beer but she's a big basketball fan. She used to play sports in high school. I tell her about my high school sports days when I used to play football and basketball. I don't tell her that I was a backup linebacker in football and only made it as far as junior varsity in basketball. Didn't want to spoil the mood. Darlene seemed interested in everything that I had to say. She was especially impressed that I had graduated college. Darlene only made it as far as high school. It's kinda nice to be around somebody who's impressed by the fact that I had been to college and was not trying to get me to go further with my education. It's a nice change of pace.

Five minutes to midnight. Everybody is standing with drinks in their hands. Darlene is really leaning into me. She's even holding my hand. I guess she likes me. Everybody is real festive now. The minutes pass quickly. We're now down to seconds. Everybody starts counting along with the host of some TV special.

"Ten! Nine! Eight! Seven! Six! Five! Four! Three! Two! One! Happy New Year!"

Darlene kisses me. Her lips feel good.

"Happy New Year," Darlene whispers in my ear as she puts arms around my neck.

"Happy New Year to you too!" She has a soft body.

We slow dance. We're so into each other I don't even know whose song is on nor do I really care. As good as Darlene feels I would dance with her even if the music wasn't playing.

****

"You have a nice apartment," Darlene says as we walk through the door of my apartment.

"It's okay."

"Did you have a nice time at the party tonight?"

"Yes I did."

I indicate the couch. "Have a seat on the couch. Take your shoes off, get comfortable."

As Darlene complies with my invitation I stick a tape of my favorite slow jams into my stereo. I sit down next to Darlene and immediately kiss her. While we're kissing she massages my neck. She certainly knows how to relax a man.

"Steve, take off your shirt and lay on your stomach," Darlene says. She watches as I take off my turtle neck and undershirt and then lay on my stomach on the couch. "You have a nice strong body. Do you work out?"

"All the time." Yes the gym membership is starting to pay off. "So what are you going to do?"

"Lay down and relax. Let me do what I have to do." Darlene straddles me. She works the muscles around my neck. Slowly, very slowly. She has strong hands. She's really getting into it. Slowly she works her way down my back. My muscles are really starting to loosen up. She keeps working and working. Finally after massaging my back for about fifteen minutes, Darlene stretches out to kiss and lick my back. After a while Darlene turns me over to kiss and lick my chest. This is feels real good. I rub her back and grab her butt like a wild man. She stops me. My first thought is that she's going to be like Tamara. She reassures me otherwise.

"Calm down Steve. Let me do what I have to do then we can do what you have to do," Darlene says in a soothing manner. I definitely think I can enjoy this woman. Definitely a happy new year.

Fourteen

I can't believe I've sunk this low. I couldn't afford the rent on my apartment so I didn't renew the lease. Too bad. I really loved the place. I had lived there for three years. Now here I am in this little efficiency on 16th St. At least it has a garage. I would really hate to park my car in the neighborhood. Lot of nice looking Hispanic babes walking through though. I've even caught a few checking me out. I guess they can't help themselves. I'm looking good as ever. I'm down to 225. Man it's hard to believe that I've lost that much weight. Even my face is starting to look different. I barely recognize myself. I've had to take a lot of suits to the tailor. My jeans are looking baggy, like the kids and whatnot. Too bad I couldn't stay in my apartment. I betcha I could really bring the women in. Funny thing is though I really haven't been chasing them. Not with Darlene around anyway. She sure knows how to take care of a man. Darlene cooks for me, gives me massages, the whole nine yards. She's almost too good to be true. Then again the way I've been looking lately any woman would want to jump my bones. Darlene is lucky to have me.

You know, the apartment isn't that bad. For a little hole in the wall. I can't believe they charge as much as they do for this place. Ah well. Beggars can't be choosers. I need to get a better job. I'm beginning to get depressed in that department. These firms haven't been calling for interviews. Not one interview. Maybe my firm blackballed me. Naw, why would they do that, especially when they said that they would provide me with excellent references? Then again it is a tough job market out there. I'm hearing about attorneys taking jobs as paralegals. They're the lucky ones. Man I just don't know. Ah well. I need to get out of here. The game is about to start and I need to get over to Ray and Ted's.

****

"I have only one word for Gary Jones, overrated!" Ted says as we're watching this college basketball game.

"He's not that bad," Ray says. "Give him a chance. You see they don't hardly give him the ball."

"Yeah Ted," I add. "Give the brother a chance. You see how the zone is collapsing on him."

"You can say what you want," Ted says. "Gary sucks. Everybody talked about how good he was coming out of high school. He must not have had that much competition."

"Why you so hard on him Ted?" I ask.

"Because he's sorry. He better get used to the letters C, B, A. Better yet, he better get used to the letters M, B, A. I hope he's hitting the books."

"He'll be all right," Ray says.

"All right?" Ted asks. "He'll be even better if he's been taking some foreign language courses because he might not be good enough for the CBA. You sure he was a McDonald's All-American when he came out of high school? It's more likely that he was all-neighborhood. The only thing that he had to do with McDonald's is that he ate there."

"You know Ted, you can really be cold sometimes," I say.

"Thanks, I really work at it," Ted grins.

"No, thank you."

The game ended with Gary Jones scoring 25 points and Ted making some feeble comment about weak competition even though the game was decided on a last second shot. We sit around after that kicking it, drinking some beers. I should have gone home because I do have to work tomorrow. Then again it's not like I do anything on my job. I sit around and chill. Which is what I'm doing now. As Ray would say, it seems like a good thing to do. We sit around talking about what men usually do when they sit around. Sports and women. In this case women.

"So how are things going between you and Darlene?" Ray asks as he's sipping his beer.

"Can't complain," I answer. "She's great in bed. All about me."

"That's a change from all your other women," Ted says. "You usually don't get that far with them."

"Dag Ted. You can't leave well enough alone," I say.

"Well...No."

"You're a cold brother sometimes."

"More like lukewarm."

"So how is Darlene?" Ray cuts in. "Outside of what she does for you in bed."

"She's alright. She's not the most intelligent woman. She's a straight around the way girl. Not at all what I'm used to dealing with,"

"I'll let that one pass," Ted says.

"So when did you get so picky?" Ray asks.

"I've always been picky," I say.

"The women have always been picky with you as well Steve," Ted says. I knew he couldn't let that one pass.

"Ya gotta have standards. I like my women to be fine with a certain level of education,"

Ted takes a swig of soda. "Standards? A couple of months ago you were a big fat slob who didn't want to further his education. Now you're a well-built slob who doesn't want to further his education."

"You're a trip Ted." I try to look like I'm not fazed by Ted's comment.

Ray chimes in. "I have to agree with Ted on this one. You really shouldn't be that hard on Darlene. She may not be a rocket scientist but she is a nice person. Besides education doesn't make you a better person. How you treat people is ultimately what matters."

"Yeah whatever." I hate when somebody tries to preach to me. Sounding like my father.

"Steve, Darlene is nice to you. You need have a better attitude towards her. If you don't you might lose a good woman."

"Darlene isn't going anywhere," I say confidently. "She's too into me for all that."

"We'll see," Ray says.

****

"That was a nice movie," Darlene says as we walk into my apartment. "I love action flicks."

I take our coats and hang them in the closet. "So do I."

"I love seeing movies like that. Sometimes I wish that I could have a life like that."

"It's all make believe. I mean how many people go through a day, kill twenty people, escape from a fiery building, drive cars at top speeds, and get the girl at the end. It's a fantasy."

"Ah Steve, don't spoil it for me. Sometimes I wish I could do more with my life. I'd like to get a more permanent job. Sometimes I think I should go to college. I'm not sure if I could make it though."

"College is pretty tough, but I got through alright."

"You sure did. A Dean's List student and all. I'd probably get bad grades if I went."

"Don't worry about college. You're doing alright for yourself. You're probably better off without college."

"Maybe, maybe I can find a man to take care of me. A college graduate. Somebody who's six feet and real built. Somebody working as a paralegal. We could get a house in some good part of town. I would cook and clean for him. Have dinner ready for him when he got home."

"Oh yeah," I rub Darlene's neck as we sit down on my couch. "What else would you have ready for him?"

Darlene kisses my cheek. "I would have a bath ready for my man so he could get all the dirt and grime off of him when he got home after a hard day's work."

"Sounds good to me." I kiss Darlene's face.

"Come on, let's open up the bed," Darlene says as we stand up to let out the bed out of the couch.

Darlene takes off my shirt and I lay down on the bed on my stomach. Darlene gets on top of me and massages my back. She starts around my neck going nice and slow. She works her way down. Man she some magic fingers. This is so chill. Darlene turns me over and we really start to go for it.

****

Sunday morning we get up and have a nice breakfast. Darlene can get down in the kitchen. I wake up to the smell of a ham and vegetable omelet. I walk the couple of feet to the kitchen/dining room. Man this apartment is small. I think I'll keep Darlene. Great in bed and can cook. What else does a man need?

Darlene is cheerful. "Good morning Steve,"

"Morning Darlene." I sit down at my kitchen table. "All this for me?"

"Of course Steve, all for you. You don't mind if I get a little do you?"

"Not at all." I motion her to sit down. Wasting no time I immediately dig in.

Darlene looks concerned. "So do you like it?"

"Mmmmmm." My mouth is full.

"I'm glad you like it," Darlene smiles.

"I didn't know that you could cook this well," I say between bites.

"I've worked at a couple of restaurants before."

"Why didn't you stick with it? You can really cook."

"I wasn't into it."

"Not exciting enough huh?"

"That and some other things."

"Other things like what?"

"I had issues with some of the people at these restaurants. Working with others can be a problem at times. Too many people think that they can get over on me. Think that they can take advantage of me. I ain't going out like that."

"Take advantage of you? Why would anybody try to do that?"

"I don't know. Maybe because I'm so nice. People always trying to get over on somebody nice."

"Any men try to get over on you?"

"All the time. This one man who I was with had the nerve to creep out on me."

"How did you find out?"

"One of my girlfriends told me."

"So what did you do?"

"I kicked him to the curb. I figured that if he couldn't stay loyal with me, treating him nice, cooking for him, making love to him, doing everything for him, I didn't really need him. I left him and never looked back."

"Wow, just like that."

"Steve," Darlene says with the most serious look on her face. "I may not be the smartest or most beautiful woman around. I may not carry myself like I'm all that. I do have common sense. I know when somebody's bad for me. I'm not like these other women out here constantly taking abuse from their men. If something's not right I leave. I'm not even going to try to work it out."

"You don't have to worry about that from me. I'll always treat you right."

"You've been doing all right so far. Keep up the good work." Darlene gives me a kiss on the cheek.

****

After finishing breakfast we went back to bed and made love again. What a way to work off the breakfast. After chilling for a little while we showered, threw on some clothes and drove out to the mall in Pentagon City. We went shopping, got something to eat, and just chilled. It was nice walking around with Darlene. I'm really starting to fall for her. What I like most is that people are looking at us and smiling. One brother even gave me a thumbs up signal when he saw me and Darlene. Yeah, I could get used to Darlene, especially after that breakfast this morning. I can't believe I'm thinking this way. I thought Darlene would be a fling. I didn't see myself actually falling for her. After all, she hasn't even been to college. She's not on my level. Ah well, I'm not going to worry about that now. I'll enjoy her company. I'll let the future take care of itself.

****

Friday night and payday. My two favorite times. Even though I'm not sure if this little something-something from my job should qualify as a paycheck. Seems like Uncle Sam and FICA are getting a little bit too much of my money. Still though, it's good to get paid. I have a little bit of extra money. I should give Darlene a big surprise this week. Let me call her. Alright, alright, pick up the phone.

Darlene picks up the phone. "Yeah?"

"Darlene, what's up?"

"Steve! What's going on?"

"Nothing much. Darlene, let's get a room at a hotel downtown. We can get room service and everything. We can make love in class."

"We can get room service and everything and maybe watch TV but we can't make love."

"Why not?"

"I'm on my period."

"Oh. Well that's alright. We can go another time."

"We can still get together tonight."

"Well since we can't go to the hotel maybe we should chill tonight. We can see each other tomorrow. When do you get off your period?"

"Around Tuesday."

"Why don't we chill out until Wednesday? We can do something then."

"I see. So what are you going to do tonight?"

"I'll probably just hang out with my boys."

"Okay. Goodbye Steve."

"Talk to you later Darlene." Darlene is so cool.

****

I'm chilling with Ray and Ted Friday tonight. We're at this club downtown. It's a trip watching these two brothers at work. Ted will walk up to any woman and start talking. 99 percent of the time he will get the number. He doesn't even try to go out with all of them. Ted says it's enough of a sport to get their phone numbers. Ted only has sex enough to keep from going stir crazy. He likens sex to eating, something that is a biological necessity. Ray on the other hand has women who walk up and buy him drinks. Usually I would watch Ray and Ted do their thing. Tonight though a lot of women are giving me some play. Going to the gym has done wonders for my love life. As if I need it. Having Darlene is enough. It was fun tonight. I get home and hit the sack.

I wake up this morning and go to the gym and have a nice long workout. I've come a long way since I first started working out. I can run a couple of miles on the track. I remember when I could run only a couple of laps. I can bench press over 200 pounds. My body is looking more cut-up. Even my face is starting to look different. I used to have fat chipmunk cheeks. Now I'm starting to get that sunken cheek look that a lot of body builders and models have. Maybe I should model. Ha ha.

I need to give Darlene a call. Hmmmm, her answering machine is on. Funny, she's usually home around this time. Dag, let me leave a message.

"Darlene, it's Steve, give me call."

I hope she calls back soon. I think I'll take a nap now

****

Oh man, that was long nap. What time is it? 8:30! Why hasn't Darlene called back? Let me call her. Dag, answering machine again.

"Darlene it's Steve again. Where are y..."

"Steve, I'm only going to say this once. Don't ever call here again," Darlene says calmly.

"Why not? What happened?"

"You think about it."

"What are..." Dag, she hung up on me. I wonder why she's stressing. Man I really liked her too. Forget her. I'll go out to a club tonight. The shape I'm in I'll have new woman by the morning. Still though, I wonder why she's acting this way. What did I do?

Thirteen

Friday night. I'd been dreading this all week. Now he's at the door. Aw well, I gotta face this like a man. As he would say. I open the door to let my father into my apartment. "Hey Pops."

"Good evening Steven," Ol' Jeremy says as he walks through my door extending his hand which I shake. Pops is a big man, 6 foot 3 and solid.

"How was the conference?" I take my father's coat and motion him to sit down on the couch.

"It was the usual. Doctors standing around telling stories and jokes that only doctors would understand. It would be good for networking if I needed that sort of thing."

That's right Pops, you make too much money to need anybody else. All you need is the money from all those rich women you play doctor with. "Why did you go?"

"I like the drive. It is fun to take the Porsche out on the open road sometimes. Just me and I-95."

"How's mom?"

"Mary is fine. As long as her students do not send her into early retirement."

"What about David and Emily?"

Pops smiles. "David is doing real well. He finally got a 3.0 GPA. I am real proud of him,"

"What about Emily?" Pops never got that happy about me making the Dean's list in college or the 3.5 average that I had throughout my college career.

"Emily could be doing better but she's trying. Teenage girls are a handful. You should see some of the clothes she tries to wear to school. I don't know about the kids these days."

"So how do you like the new apartment?"

Pops' face frowns a bit. "It is certainly small. And the neighborhood leaves a lot to be desired. The...element around here is questionable."

"It's alright around here."

"Still son, you should be living in a better environment than this. I did not raise you to live in some poor neighborhood with a bunch of foreigners."

"This neighborhood isn't that bad. A lot of professionals live around here."

"Many poor ...people as well."

"Whatever." I hate when he gets like this.

"That is your usual attitude is it not? "Whatever." That is why you are in this little rat trap. If you had a better attitude you would probably have a house and family by now."

"Come on Pops, don't get started."

"Yes son, I am going to get started. Your mother and I did not raise you to go backwards. You did so well in high school and college. You should have an advanced degree by now. What are you doing with your life? Probably getting drunk every night and chasing some of these loose women who are running the streets. You mother and I raised you better than this."

"Why are you always on me Pops? I'm doing alright?"

"Moving from a big apartment to a small apartment is all right? Losing a job you have been on for five years is all right? What is wrong with you son?"

"Nothing's wrong with me! I'm doing better than a lot of people out there. At least I'm not in prison, or on drugs, or unemployed. Doesn't that count for something?"

"You are not in prison, on drugs, or unemployed because I would like to think that your mother and I raised you better than that. I would hope that you would not even want to sink to that level."

"I won't Pops. I won't go that low."

"It is 'I will not go that low.' Son, you can do better."

"Whatever."

"Have you a least been going to church?"

"No."

"Why not? You have not found a church home?"

"I'm not sure about God."

"What are you not sure of son?"

"Whether he exists."

"I see why you have fallen so far."

"I haven't fallen that far Pops."

"Your mother and I did not raise you to not to believe in God."

"That's just it. You tried to force God on me. I need to find out for myself."

"If you do not know God has blessed you so far in your life I do not know what to say about you."

"You know Pops, I think you're a hypocrite. You talk about God this and God that, yet God doesn't stop you from talking about poor people, especially those who're Black. It doesn't stop you from looking down on them. God didn't stop you from having those affairs with all those women. What do you have to say to that?"

"None of us are perfect son. We can only beg forgiveness and try to do our best," Pops says with a sad look.

"Whatever. Pops I have a date tonight. You're welcome to stay here."

"That is all right Steven. Time for me to get up the road anyway." Pops stands up to get his coat and hat.

"Tell mom and David and Emily I said hi."

"Okay son. Keep in mind everything that I said." With that Pops leaves. No handshake, no hugs, nothing. Like he's always been.

I lied about having a date tonight. I just wanted my father out of my apartment. Asshole.

****

One of the bad things about my current job is that they don't have parking. So every morning I have to take the bus to work. The bus ride is usually an adventure. All sorts of characters get on board. Everything from a young business executive to a homeless person. Most of the time I get a good seat on the bus. Usually sitting next to somebody or standing up, crushed by two or three people. Today is a good day. I got a seat by the window. Everything's going alright today so far. Hmmmm, there's a fine woman at the bus stop. I hope she sits next to me. Which she is doing! My lucky day. What an opportunity. I can't let this one get away.

"Good morning," I say to the woman. She has a smooth mocha complexion with long black wavy hair. She looks like she could be mixed. She has the most amazing brown eyes.

She smiles. "Good morning,"

"Are you all ready for work this fine Monday morning?"

"Not really. I wish this was a three day weekend."

"Busy weekend?"

"You could say that."

I extend my hand. "My name is Steve by the way."

"Candace, pleased to meet you."

"This is the first time I've seen you on the bus. I would remember somebody as attractive as you."

Candace blushed. "I usually go to work on a later bus."

"So where do you work?"

109

"I work at an accounting firm on K Street. I'm an administrative assistant. What do you do?"

"I'm a paralegal at a litigation support company."

"Sounds interesting."

"Trust me, it's not."

"You never know what I might find interesting," Candace says suggestively.

"Candace, I know this is forward of me, but I would like to get to know you better. You have a number I can reach you at?"

"I'll write it down for you." Candace reaches into her purse and gets out a notepad to write down her phone number. "Why don't you give me a call tonight? We can talk more. My stop is coming up."

"Thanks. I'll definitely give you a call." I get her phone number and watch her get off the bus. She looks like she has a nice body under that coat.

****

I gave Candace a call that night. Interestingly, she's 35 years old. She's seven years older than me. I turned 28 only a few weeks ago. I'm a true Aquarius. As if there were any fake ones. Candace is an interesting person. She has a couple of years of college. She likes to work out even though she's probably ten pounds overweight which is alright since she's still good-looking. Only problem is that she has a boyfriend. Must not matter to her because we're still going to see a movie tonight. We've been talking all week. We're going to see this movie called *Perceptions*. Supposed to be pretty good. We'll see. I certainly hope Candace is pretty good after the movie.

****

Candace lives about five minutes driving distance from my apartment, just off of 16th street. She looks good when I pick her up. She has on a long black overcoat over a tight sweater and jeans. I hope they are not too hard to get off. We make small talk on the way to the movie.

"I heard that this was a good movie. Very funny," Candace says.

"What's the movie about?"

"It's about this man who different people see in different ways. Some people see him as a nerd while some see him as a stud while others see him as a jock and so on.

"Sounds like a winner."

"I can't wait to see it."

"So what did you tell your boyfriend about tonight?"

"I told him that I was going to hang out with my girlfriends tonight."

"He bought that?"

"He believes everything I tell him. He's like that."

"He trusts you totally?"

"Yes, that's why I'm with him. He's so sweet."

"You're stepping out on him though."

"He's sweet but boring. A girl has got to have some fun."

"I guess I'm fun then?"

"You are fine. You're so smart and muscular. I could tell you lifted weights the first time I saw you. I like muscular men."

"And I like fine women." I'm thinking past the movie to when I take Candace back to my apartment.

We talk about this and that on the rest of drive to the movie theater.

****

The movie was pretty good. There was some good acting. The only problem with the movie was my date. She kept talking through the whole film. Yelling at the screen and everything. It was embarrassing to be sitting with a 35 year-old woman who was yelling at the screen, laughing too loud, and generally being obnoxious. It got so bad that some of the teenagers in the theater were looking at her funny. I was glad the film ended. I was ready to out of there the way Candace was acting. I guess age and maturity do not necessarily go hand in hand.

****

"So this is your place? I like it. It's cute," Candace says as we walk through the door of my apartment.

I hang up our coats. "It'll do for now. I used to have a bigger place on Wisconsin Ave. I want to get back over there."

"You just got into this apartment. Give it some time. You'll grow to like it," Candace says as she sits down on my couch.

I bring out some red wine and a couple of glasses. I pour Candace some wine. She takes a sip.

"I like this wine," she says.

I sit down next to her. "I'm glad you do. Let me put on some music." I use the remote control to turn on the tape and a Barry White song comes on.

"Oooh you're a fan of Barry's."

"Sure you're right." I take the wine glasses and put them on the coffee table.

I lean over to kiss Candace. She put her arms around my neck and squeezes tightly. Slowly we take off each other's clothes and have sex right there on the couch.

****

"Thanks for the evening." Candace is getting ready to step out of my car to go to her apartment. "I had a nice time."

The way you were yelling at the movie and on the couch I'm glad you did. "I'm glad you enjoyed the evening."

"We have to do this again."

"We certainly do."

Candace gives me a good night kiss. "Give me a call."

"I'll do that." The requisite lie.

After watching Candace walk into her building I drive home to get some sleep. I've already decided not to call Candace anymore. She's fine and everything. Good sex. She's not the type of woman that I could get involved with for anything outside of sex. A woman that would easily fool around on her boyfriend would just as easily fool around on me as well. No problem, I'll just find another playmate.

Twelve

"Ray, you seem to know where all the parties are. What's your secret?" I'm driving out to a party in Rockville with Ray riding shotgun.

"Just how it is."

"This brother out here rich or what?"

"Kevin? Nope. He's having the party at his sister's place. Her husband is rich. Big-time surgeon and whatnot."

"There's going to be some honeys out here?"

"There should be."

"I hope so, I'm ready to pick up some new women, especially after that wacked babe Candace."

"Whatever."

Ray is acting kinda distant. I wonder what's up. "How come Ted isn't out here with us? I actually miss his bama ass making fun of me."

"You know Ted. He has a woman coming over. He's going to microwave a dinner for her, sweet talk her, and then do the do on the futon."

"Ted has so much class."

"Speaking of class, Darlene told me what you did. It was real low."

Now what? "What did I do?"

"You don't know what you did?"

"Apparently not." I wish he would tell me.

"I talked to Darlene last night. She told me about that night a while ago you hung out with me and Ted. I was wondering why you wanted to hang with us instead of Darlene."

"I didn't tell you? Darlene was on her period that night. I didn't see the point of hanging with her so I decided to hang with you and Ted. Only thing, Darlene was bugging about something. For some reason she doesn't want to talk to me anymore."

"Steve, you must be the biggest fool I know. Not only do you waste your intelligence but you don't have any common sense."

"What the hell are you talking about?"

"Of course she's "bugging" Steve. You basically let her know in so many words that she is only good for sex."

I try to pay attention to Ray and the road. "I didn't do that."

"Think for once Steve. You didn't want to go out with her because she was on her period."

"So?"

"So? I can see why the women are falling all over you," Ray says sarcastically.

I mask my growing anger. "What are you talking about?"

"Steve, I thought you said that you liked Darlene."

"I did."

"I thought you liked her beyond sex."

"I did. She's a good cook and all. She's fun to be around."

"Steve, don't you see? You hurt her feelings with your actions."

"I didn't hurt her. She was on her period. What else were we to do?"

"Has everything become sex to you?"

"I gotta get mine. Besides look who's talking. Mr. "girl for every night." As big a dog as you are."

"Despite what you may believe I have never dogged a woman. I treat every woman with respect. I make every one of them feel special."

"Whatever. Look, we're here." We drive by the house where the party is going on.

"Steve, you need to change your attitude towards women. One day you're going to meet that one woman who's going to leave your heart in a trash can."

I shake my head and bug my eyes at Ray. "That ain't gonna happen aw'ight."

"You're a fool sometimes."

The party is alright so far. There's a good mix of people in here. Old and young. Bourgeois and down. Beautiful and ugly.

People are mixing and dancing. As soon as Ray walks through the door the women jumped all over him. I guess he'll be "nice" to all of them. Hypocrite. One thing, women are checking me out more than ever. Must be the body. I'm down to 210. I keep working, I'll be down to 200. Then the women will really be on me. Too bad there aren't more beautiful women here. The ones that are here have men all over them. Aw well, I'll chill out for a little while. In fact this beer is kinda low. Time for a refill. I head for the kitchen to fill up. It looks like this brother has the same idea.

"Nice party." I reach into the refrigerator to get a beer. "You want one cuz?"

"You read my mind," Cuz says.

"This alright?" I hand him a beer.

"Any beer is a good beer. There's some nice gals in here tonight."

Gals? "Yeah they're in here but I've been to parties where all the women look good."

"The ugly ones need loving too." Cuz looks around like a lion surveying a herd of antelope.

"Gotta have standards though."

"My friend, a gal is a gal."

"You sound like this guy I used to work with. He used to love ugly women."

"No women are ugly, especially in the dark."

"You might have point there."

Cuz extends his hand. "My name is Samuel by the way."

"Steve." I shake Samuel's hand.

"What do you do?"

"I work as a paralegal downtown. Yourself."

"This and that. I have a lot things going. I own a couple of vending stands. Selling everything from books to perfumes. I really make a lot of money from T-Shirts, especially since it's starting to get warmer out."

"It must be nice owning a business. Easy work."

"It's anything but easy. It is satisfying. I couldn't keep working for other people. It wasn't me. I saved up some money and decided to go into business for myself."

"Whatever works."

"You ever do any vending?"

"No."

"Tell you what. Here's my card. If you ever need a job give a call," Samuel says as he hands his business card to me.

I get my wallet out and put the card in. "Thanks man."

"No problem Steve. It was good meeting you. Right now the hunt is on." Samuel walks over to a rather plump woman.

I need to find a woman to talk to and seduce. All the fine ones are taken. Wait, who's tapping me on my shoulder.

"Hi, you don't look like you're enjoying yourself," the woman says.

I shrug my shoulder. "The party's alright." The woman is short and fat around the middle. She looks to be in her late thirties to early forties. She has that look in her eye.

"I've watched you walk around. You haven't really hooked up with anybody. Now I'm thinking that this man is too fine to be standing by himself. So I figure I'd just come over here and see what's going on with you. My name is Janet by the way."

"Steve. I'm alright though. You don't have to worry about me."

"Everybody should have somebody to worry about them," Janet says as she rubs my arm.

"Really?" Ol' girl is flirting with me. I don't know though, she's old and fat. That's not a good combination. Hold up, this dude is coming over here like he knows her. Maybe he's her boyfriend.

"Hey Janet," Cuz says, looking very dorky. Cuz has fat cheeks and a skinny body. Looks about 45. "This one of your co-workers?"

"No Tim, I just met him tonight. Tim, this is Steve. Steve, Tim.

"Yo, what's up man?" Cuz ain't even trying to shake my hand.

"You enjoying the party man?" Tim asks. He looks like I'm invading his territory.

"It's aw'ight." Maybe if I get a little "street" on him he'll chill out. I don't feel like any problems.

"Tim, why don't you go get us something to drink. I'll be in with you in a second," Janet says.

"Okay, nice meeting you," Tim says as he turns to leave.

"Likewise."

Janet looks embarrassed. "Sorry about that. Tim thinks he's my boyfriend sometimes."

"He's not your boyfriend?"

"No, he's just a good friend. He drove me and my girlfriends down here from Hagerstown."

"Is that right?"

"I'd like to talk to you again Steve. Maybe we can go out. Can you remember phone numbers?"

"Depends on the ink in the pen."

"You're going to have to remember this one. Tim's looking over this way. Write it down in the bathroom or something. It's 301-555-5467. Give me a call. I would like to go out with you."

"Would you?" She must be kidding. I guess she wants cuz to come hunt me down. Janet isn't fine enough for all that.

"I know what I like. Talk to you soon." Janet walks over to Tim.

I'm not calling this skeezer. "Yeah, soon." The requisite lie.

I've danced with a couple of women. Both average looking. Ray's doing a lot better than I am. I guess it's because he's so "nice." If cuz wasn't built like crazy he would be lonely. Like women want him for his personality. Man, this is the worst party I've ever been to. I haven't picked up anybody. Wait, Janet. Naw, I still haven't picked up anybody. I probably couldn't "pick up" Janet anyway. She has a whole lot around her stomach. Aw well. Let me get something to eat. Hmmmm, who's this over by the food. Nice phat ass. Alright baby turn around. Turn around. Turn...oops. Turn back baby. With your face I bet a lot of men do you doggy style.

"Hi," The woman says.

"How ya doing? Enjoying the party?" She does have a nice body. Even the face can't take away from that.

"It's good. Even better now," the woman flirts.

Must be the cologne. "My name's Steve."

"Anna."

"Have you been here long?"

"No I got here a little while ago with my girlfriends. We're coming from another party. That one was dead."

"So this one is better?"

Anna looks me up and down. "In one respect it is." She isn't even trying to be subtle about it.

"So what do you do for fun?"

"I usually go to different clubs. I go to an occasional cabaret. Do you go to cabarets?"

"Not really. I go to a club every now and then. I prefer going to house parties. I like going to the movies."

"Do you work out?"

"Yes. How can you tell?" I try to sound modest.

"You have a great body."

"Do I?"

"Yes you do. Don't be so modest about it."

I'm not. "Thanks."

"I usually work out five or six days a week. I lift weights and run on the indoor track."

"You're certainly get good results. I need to work out more. Lose this weight."

"You look great. You don't need to lose any weight. You have a great figure." Your face on the other hand...

"Thank you. You're so sweet. Would you like to dance?"

"Sure why not."

So we're dancing. She can move that nice ol' butt of hers. Yeah, shake it baby.

I dance and talk with Anna the rest of the night. Not so much because I'm interested in her, but because quite frankly no one else is around. We exchange numbers before I leave. I leave by myself because Ray finds some woman to take him home. I guess it's because he's so "nice" to the ladies. Anyway it was a subpar night. Then again I shouldn't expect every party to be kicking.

Eleven

"Steve, you have done a good job for us." Kathleen says as I'm sitting in her office. Work had been slowing down lately. Everybody figured that there would be a massive amount of layoffs. After all, it was only a temp project.

"Thank you." Bend over, here it comes.

"However, due to the amount of work that we have, we no longer require the number of staff that we are carrying."

"I understand."

"There were some decisions that were made. Unfortunately, we are going to have to let some people go. We have decided not to renew your contract."

"Will you be keeping anybody?"

"We are holding a few people over. We have other things for them."

Hold up, Kathleen is going to have to explain this to me. "Why am I being let go? I thought I was doing a good job."

"Quite frankly Steve, your work was adequate at best."

"Adequate? I can digest in my sleep. I used to digest all the time at the firm I used to work at."

"I'm not sure about the work you did at the firm, but your work here was not that great. Your overall performance was adequate. There were, however, several areas of concern to us."

"What areas?"

"For one thing, your production rate was fair at best. Productivity is the name of the game in this business. Then there's the matter of all the socializing you did around here when you should have been working. Finally, there have been several times where you have been observed daydreaming. Steve, this is not a college classroom. This is a business. The litigation support business. We get paid for productivity. If we are not productive we do not get paid. It is that simple. We cannot have workers who are not productive. You should keep that in mind when you search for your next job."

"Yes, I will keep that in mind." Bitch.

I get up and walk out of Kathleen's office without saying anything else to her. I expected to be laid off. She didn't have to say the things she said though. Forget her. I'll show her. I'll get a better job. I wonder what happened with Dwayne and Stephanie. They're talking when I get back to our space.

"Yo they gave me the boot," I say.

"I got fired too," Stephanie says. "I'm not worried about it. I just signed with a temp agency where one of my girlfriends works. She told me that they're real good about finding work for people."

"What about you Dwayne?" I ask.

"I will still be here. They have another project starting on Monday. God has blessed me to keep working. I give him praise every day."

Again with God. "I needed to get out of here. I wasn't making enough money."

"You have any job prospects lined up Steve?" Stephanie asked.

"Of course not. If I did I wouldn't be here."

"You don't have to say it like that Steve."

"I'm sorry if I sounded harsh, Stephanie."

"That's all right Steve. It's always tough to be fired."

"Laid off you mean."

"Fired. My father always told me to call something for what it is. He told me to always face the truth no matter how harsh it may be."

"The Bible says the truth shall set you free," Dwayne adds.

"Whatever." I try not sound to irritated.

"Steve," Stephanie says, probably sensing the tension. "For what it's worth it was great working with you. Had some good times."

"Same here, Stephanie. I'm not going to have anybody to flirt with and get my heart broken."

"Poor baby. We can still keep in touch."

"The invitation to church is still open for both of you," Dwayne says.

"Thanks," Stephanie responds. "I have to take you up on that one day."

"I don't know Dwayne. I haven't really gone to church since college. It's not me," I say.

"That's all right Steve. One day it will be you."

"Whatever."

We clean up our stuff and finished the day out. I'm really glad to be leaving that company. I'll never work there again. Productivity. Give me a break.

****

Wednesday. I have the resume out but I haven't really heard from anybody. I'm not really going to stress about it. Gives me time to catch up on the talk shows and to spend more time in the gym. My weight is down to 200. I'm really pumping now. Women are starting to come up and start conversations. Women are blatantly flirting with me. What a good life. Now if I can only get a job. Ah well, right now I'll just chill on the exercise bike. Just me and the workout tape that Ted made for me. Cuz can mix some music. Hey, here comes Darryl. "Yo Darryl! What's up cuz?"

"How are you Steve?"

"Alright. Even though I lost my job on last week."

"It was a temp job anyway, right?"

"Yeah."

"Did you learn anything from the job?"

"Not really."

"I have problems believing that sir. We learn from every experience positive or negative. We just don't recognize this all the time."

"You're a wise brother Darryl. You were probably a good kid."

"No, not really, but that's a story for another day. Maybe I'll share it with you over a couple of brews."

"I look forward to that."

"How's the job search going?"

"Slow, real slow. I have some savings but they're running out real fast."

"Steve, if you want a job believe that you have the job. Once you set that in your mind you will get results."

"I'll keep that in mind. Still, I kinda wish that I'd never got laid off my job at the law firm."

"I know you miss the money and everything that came with it but you never know, it may have been the best thing that happened to you."

"What do you mean?"

"Being laid off might have been the best thing for you. It might have been the thing that will help you grow."

"I don't get you Darryl."

"I'll give you an example Steve. A man has a plant that grows best outdoors in the sun. The man, however, keeps the plant indoors by the window. Now the plant gets plenty of sunlight by the window but it will only grow so much because it belongs outside. Inside the plant may grow a foot. Outside the plant may grow into a tree."

"I think I understand what you're saying. Being at the firm may have prevented me from growing. Thing is, I was content to stay at that level."

"Some people are meant to stay at one level because they simply refuse to grow. Others will grow at a snail's pace while others at a horse's pace. I've talked with you and watched you around here. You're definitely meant to grow."

"You think so."

"You'll see," Darryl says with that always wise look in his eyes.

"You're a fascinating brother Darryl."

"I'm just a man who was forced to learn life's lessons. I have to get back to my workout. Talk to you later bro."

Darryl is something.

****

Darryl's a deep man. He gave me a lot to think about as I drive home. I need to get off my ass and find a job. I have an idea. I should have a thought about this earlier.

****

"Hello Samuel. This is Steve from the party the other week." I decided to give Samuel a call.

"How are you Steve? I was wondering if you were going to call."

"Samuel, I'll get right to the point. I need a job. You have anything?"

"Initiative. I like that. As a matter of fact I do have something. There's going to be an expo at a hotel this coming Saturday. I'm going to have a couple of booths there. I could use some extra people. You'll be at the booth with me."

"What are we selling?"

"A little bit of everything. Books, shirts, incense. I expect to make a lot of money."

"You have anything beyond that?"

"We'll see how you do Saturday. If you do all right, we'll see what we can do."

"That's cool"

"Tell you what, Steve. Give me a call Friday evening so I can finalize everything with you."

"What do you want me to wear?"

"Just be clean. Nothing crazy. This is a business so come ready to work. Just do me that solid."

"Okay Samuel. You'll hear from me on Friday evening. Talk to you then." I hang up the phone. Alright I have a job just like that.

****

This is some stuff. A couple of weeks ago I was sitting around thinking about how boring my digesting job was and now

I'm in this hotel ballroom trying to sell some products along with Samuel and these two women, Adele and Fay. Both are extraordinarily average looking. They're in no danger of me hitting on them. This is so chilled though. I stand here and tell people how much something costs. I take their money and give them the product. This is alright even though I've been here for a couple of hours and we've only picked up a few sales. Samuel has only spent a little time at his two tables. He's been walking around mostly to network with other vendors. I'll let him network, I'll chill. There's some fine women in here.

"Steve, stop watching the booty walk by. How are the sales going?" Samuel asks. I didn't even see him approach me.

"Slow. Only a few people have stopped by the table and then only a couple have bought anything."

"Steve I've been watching you for a little while. You're too passive. Watch me." Samuel looks around for a second. "Watch this."

"Excuse me," Samuel motions to a couple that is walking past the booth. "Come check out what we have."

Amazingly the couple comes right over. Average looking Joes. They look like a good couple because they look just alike. Ordinary.

"You are such a beautiful couple," Samuel says as he starts his pitch. "May I interest you in some lotions? I would suggest this cocoa butter lotion."

"I don't know." The man shows reluctance to buy anything.

"This lotion is very good for massages," Samuel speaks more to the woman than the man. "Smell this."

Samuel opens the container and allows the woman to take a sniff.

"How do you like it?" Samuel asks the woman.

"Smells good."

Samuel continues his pitch. "Now think about it. You and your man have a nice romantic evening. He can rub this into his hand and give you a nice soothing massage."

"I don't know about this," the man says.

"Quiet Elmo," the woman says. "I'll take two."

Samuel looks satisfied. "That'll be ten dollars,"

After the couple left Samuel turns to me with a smile on his face. "You see Steve, you just have to be aggressive about sales. You can't wait for them to come to you. You have to bring them over. Then you have to convince them that they need your product. Works best with the gals. Most of them came here to spend money anyway. You just have to convince them to spend money on your products. Now you try it. I have to go over to the bathroom real quick." Samuel leaves for the bathroom.

A minute later a beautiful woman walks up to look at the books on the table. I decide to be more aggressive.

"That's a good book right there. Local author."

The woman is indifferent. "That's nice,"

"The main character is a strong beautiful woman such as yourself. My name is Steve by the way. You are..."

"Tracy."

"Well hello Tracy. This is a nice book. A lot of single women enjoyed it. You'll probably enjoy it.

"Are you trying to find out if I'm single? Are you trying to pick me up?" Tracy is harsh.

"Oh no, I'm just trying to point out the merits of this book."

"I can read the back of the book to figure that out. I don't need you to tell me about the book."

"So would you like to buy it?"

"From you? No way. Not with you trying to hit on me."

"I wasn't trying to hit on you. You're stressing for nothing."

"I don't have to take this. I can get the book from somebody else." Tracy puts the book down and walks away.

"Well get it from somewhere else then," I say loud enough for her to hear me. Unfortunately, she wasn't the only one.

"What was that all about?" Samuel asks as he gets to the table.

"You saw that?"

"Yep."

"I thought you were going to the bathroom?"

"I told you that because I wanted to see how you would do without me around. It doesn't look like you're good at sales."

"Well cuz, I never sold anything in my life. I thought I told you that."

"You did. I still didn't think it would be a problem."

"It's not. That woman had an attitude."

"Whether she did or not she's still a paying customer. It didn't help that you were looking at her like she was lunch."

"Whatever."

"Whatever? Whatever? I'll tell you whatever," Samuel says as he reaches into his pocket to get out a roll of bills. "Here's thirty dollars. I don't need you or your attitude. I'm trying to make some money here."

"You're going to let me go based on one incident?"

"You've had an attitude since you got here this morning and quite frankly I don't have to deal with it. Thank you for your time."

I get my jacket to leave. "Man forget you. I didn't want to sell your crap anyway."

"You need to work on your attitude," Samuel says.

I walk away. "Whatever." I didn't like doing this anyway.

Ten

Unemployment sucks. At least I have unemployment checks coming in. For all the good it's doing me. I'm still going through my savings a little too fast. I have to find a job. The resume is still out there. Maybe somebody will give me a call. Maybe not. I have to do something. Ah man what to do? Here it is Saturday night and I'm home with no place to go. Don't really feel like going out though. No women to call up. Ray and Ted are hanging out with some ladies. Double date or something like that. I thought only high school kids did that. Nothing to do but sit here and watch TV and drink beer. I hope something good is on.

This movie is stupid. I thought Hollywood was supposed to be more creative than this. Ted needs to analyze this movie. Wait the phone. "Hello."

It's a woman. "May I speak to Steve?"

"Speaking. Who's this?"

"Steve, it's Anna. We met at that party a few weeks ago. You remember."

"Anna? Anna? Oh yeah I remember. I wanted to call you but I misplaced your phone number." The requisite lie.

"I was wondering why you haven't called me."

I didn't call because I really wasn't interested. "I was hoping you'd call me. I thought you forgot about me."

"Oh no that wasn't the case. I've been busy. I thought I would give you a call and see what you're doing tonight."

"Nothing. Just chilling, watching a movie."

"How would you like to go out tonight?"

"Would be nice but I'm broke. I was laid off my job a few weeks ago. I'm living on savings and unemployment now."

"Don't worry about anything. I'll take care of it. I know where a cabaret is out in Riverdale. I'll treat you."

"You will? Fine. I can't say no to that."

"Why don't you get ready and I'll pick you up in about an hour."

"You'll drive too? I'm honored."

"Least I can do. I'll call you to get your address before I leave. See you soon."

"Yeah later."

****

Ol' girl picks me up in a late model Toyota. Nice car. Anna works at a bank out in Maryland where she also has a townhouse.

She said this cabaret is being given by a friend of a friend. That's cool. We drive to the place making small talk. She's divorced with a son and daughter. Her kids are with their grandparents. Anna doesn't get to go out much because of her children. She's really looking forward to having a good time tonight. We get to the place and get a table with some other people. Man, there's some straight up bamas in here. Anna and I dance after being there for about fifteen minutes. Anna can move her stuff. Shaking her phat ass all over the place. Ah man. We sit down after a few songs.

"Are you all right?" She squeezes my shoulder as we sit.

I wipe the sweat away from my forehead. "I have to catch my breath. You were wearing me out. You can dance."

"Are you having a good time?"

"Can't say it's been bad."

Anna rubs my thigh for a few seconds. I wonder what's on her mind. "I'm glad."

"Reach up a little more and you might find a big surprise waiting for you."

Anna looks me in the eye. "I can't wait to find out,"

"I can't wait for you to find out." She's ugly, but with a couple of beers...

****

We leave after a little while and go to this reggae club in D.C. We get there and start dancing as soon as we walk through the door. It seems like everybody in here is grinding. Watching people dance to reggae is a trip. The women look like they're in their own world. The men dance slowly with looks on their faces like they've had some good weed.

Anna and I are out on the floor swaying to the beat when she put her arms around me and kisses me. She puts her tongue all the way down my throat. Ol' girl is really going for it. I guess she know what she wants. She did pay for the evening.

Anna takes me back to her place. We're not in there for a minute before she starts taking off my clothes. We have sex right there on the living room floor. Anna is wild. She act like she hasn't had sex for years. We have sex in the living room, the kitchen, and then finally make it to the bedroom. We get to sleep about six in the morning. We wake up about twelve and started having sex again. This woman is wearing me out. Finally she takes me home.

"Did you have a nice time?" Anna asks as she stops in front of my building.

"You can say that." I'm relieved that I'm finally home.

"Tell you what sweetie. I'll give you a call soon."

"What about this weekend?" I asked anxiously.

"I'll be busy this weekend and the next. I have some things to do with my family. I'll give you a call when I'm free." Anna leans over to give me a hard and deep tongue kiss.

I get out of the car. "See you later."

I watch Anna pull off and then head up to my apartment to throw on some gym clothes and head to the gym. For some reason I have plenty of energy.

****

I'm at the gym lifting when Darryl walks on the floor.

"Hey bro. What's up?"

"Darryl man, I feel fired up. This woman took me out last night and paid for everything. We went to this cabaret and then to this club. Then she took me to her house and worked me. I mean she worked me cuz. She dropped me off at my place a little while ago."

"Let me guess. She's in her mid to late thirties with a couple of kids."

"Yeah that's right. How did you know?"

"You forget who you're talking to sometimes bro. Women who get to a certain level in life know what they want and are aggressive about getting it. They're past the age where they feel the need to play games with men."

"Darryl, I've said it once and I'll say it a thousand times, you're one wise brother."

"As I've said before I keep my eyes open and use my brain. One thing I will say. You don't need to play games with this woman because she's above that. Trust me."

"I'll keep that in mind."

"Now if you will excuse me sir, I have to get started on my workout. Take it easy bro." Darryl walks away.

Darryl's the man. Cuz seems like he was born wise.

****

"Steve got used," Ted laughs after I tell him and Ray about my evening with Anna the night before.

"She took your stuff Steve," Ray laugh as well.

Ted is cracking up. "I bet she said she would call you."

"You think she still respects you?" Ray asks.

"Hold up, I see the scene now. The woman was on top yelling, "Whose dick is this?! Whose dick is this?!" Steve was like, "Take it! Take it! It's yours!" She probably made Steve say her name," Ted says.

I shake my head. "Okay, Okay, it wasn't all that. Dag with friends like you two,"

"Just joning on you. It's a sign that we like you. You should worry when we don't mess with you," Ray says when he stops laughing.

"Yeah Steve," Ted adds. "We do this because we love you. Syke."

"Dag Ted why do you play me?"

"Because you're easy to play."

Ray changes the subject. "Speaking of which…Steve, I have to give it to you. I didn't think you would lose the weight. I thought you were just going to sham like you always do and stay fat."

"Thanks for the vote of confidence."

"My pleasure," Ray responds. "Hey Ted get the phone."

"Yes master," Ted picks up the cordless phone. "Debbie, what's up?"

Ted takes the phone into his bedroom and closes the door.

"So Steve, how's the job search going?" Ray asks.

"It's going."

"You haven't heard from anybody?"

"Nope."

"Well, hang in there. If you had a law degree you could probably have your own practice."

"Had to get that in there, didn't you."

"Somebody has to stay on you. How long are you going to survive like this? You have to have something better in today's world. College degrees just don't mean as much as they used to back in the day."

"You're right about that. While Anna was going up and down on me I thought about a career I could get into."

"What's that?"

"I could become a gigolo."

"Stop playing Steve."

"I'm serious Ray."

"How did you come up with this great thought?"

"I figure there are thousands of women with a little bit of money who would gladly pay for companionship and sex."

"You're right but still...I hope you're joking. You must be out of your mind to even think of something like this."

"I don't know Ray. This unemployment stuff is for the birds. I don't know what to do. Sitting at home is cool sometimes but there's only so much to do. I don't think I can take it anymore."

"Tell you what. There's going to be a reception for business school candidates this Wednesday. Tag along. You might not want to go to law school but you may like the idea of going to business school. There'll be some nice women there."

"What the hell. I have nothing to do anyway."

"Be sure and wear a suit. This is a classy crowd."

"You act like I don't have good sense sometimes."

"You don't."

Nine

So here I am at this business school reception. Some school in New York is making a presentation and accepting applications. I came to eat. I did get to see another side of Ray. I guess the side I always saw was that athletic, womanizing, laid back side. Been that way ever since I met him out on a basketball court when I first came to D.C. Wonders never cease. Cuz is all businesslike and aggressive now. Talking with all the right people. I've make small talk with a few people. I honestly haven't been that friendly. I'm not here to make friends, I'm here to eat. One thing, this white girl keeps looking at me and smiling. She looks alright. Nice legs. She definitely looks interested. Wouldn't you know it? Here she comes. I guess she wants some celery dip.

"Hi," I say as I watch her get a piece of celery.

"Hi. You seem to be just standing here. Are you enjoying yourself?"

"To be honest with you, I came here to eat. So in that respect I'm enjoying myself."

"That's funny. My name's Lisa."

"Steve."

"Did you come to see what the school has to offer?"

"Naw. I really did come to eat. My buddy is getting an MBA and he came to check out the school. I think he wants to go beyond an MBA."

"I'm here to check out the school."

"Are you interested so far?"

"Maybe. I'm still checking out some schools. Steve, do you work out?" Lisa asks as she looks at my chest.

I smile. "Yes I do."

"How much do you bench press?"

"About 225."

"Fantastic. You look like you lift. How often do you work out?"

"I work out about six days a week."

"That's good. I work out 4 days a week. I would like to get in there more so I can tone up."

"You look like you're in great shape."

"Thank you. I really work at it."

"Maybe we can work out together one day."

"That would be nice."

"You like the movies."

"I love movies."

"I know this is forward of me but *Smokers* is coming out this weekend. How would you like to see it with me?"

"I would love to. I'll write my phone number down for you. I'll just put it on this note pad for you," Lisa reaches into her purse to get a note pad. She writes her number down and hands it to me.

"Thanks, I'll give you a call," I say as I look at her number.

"Well, Steve, I have to leave now. Have to get up for work tomorrow."

"Let me walk you to the door."

"Okay."

I walk Lisa out to the front of the hotel where she gets a cab to take her home. I go back to the reception to finish eating.

****

Saturday night is finally here. I've talked to Lisa a couple of times since the reception. She is a supervisor at some weird government agency. She's also 33. What's with me and all these older women lately? What happened to the good ol' days when the women I met were around my age? Lisa was alright to talk to. She seemed to make a point of telling me how many Black friends she has. Like I'm really concerned about them. I guess she was trying to let me know that she's cool with going out with me. Ah well. I went through the usual dating ritual. Got a nice jacket. It was kinda cool out despite being April. I drive out to Virginia to pick Lisa up. She is waiting at the door of her apartment building when I get there. We make small talk on the way to the theater. She tells me about her week at work and what she's been doing at the gym. I tell her what I've been doing at the gym and about my job search.

One thing that impressed me about her was that she didn't act funny when I told her that I was unemployed. A sister wouldn't have given me the time of day if I told one that I'm unemployed. A lot of brothers have said that white women are more accepting of a Black man's condition. I never really got into that stuff though. I think all those stereotypes are for the birds but who knows, there may be some truth in what is being said.

The movie was alright. It was a science fiction flick about all these beautiful people being rounded up simply because they were beautiful. They have some weird movies out there. After the film Lisa and I go to get a bite to eat at the food court of the shopping mall where we saw the movie.

"So did you like the movie?" I ask Lisa before taking a bite of the turkey sandwich I bought for myself.

"I thought it was funny."

"A lot of action though. The sight of fashion models trying to act was funny in itself."

"I think the film was meant to be a satire of society's preoccupation with physical appearance."

"There were some beautiful people in the movie, especially the women."

"The men looked pretty good too."

"All in all it was a good time. I would like to do it again sometimes."

"Steve, I've been meaning to say something. I don't know how to say it."

"Are you going to tell me that you have a boyfriend?" I'm half joking.

"No I don't have a boyfriend although I am looking for that someone special."

"So what's up?"

"Like I said I'm looking for someone special. Steve you're a nice and attractive man but I don't think we should see each other again."

"Why not?" Now what?

"It isn't because you're Black or anything. It's just that I'm looking for somebody with...a more stable employment history."

"You don't want to go out again because I'm unemployed?"

"That's right."

"But I explained my situation to you."

"You did and I sympathize. Yet I need more stability. I want to get married and have a family. I want a man who makes as much money as I do. I want a man who has some ambition. A man who wants to go as high as I want to go."

Where have I heard that before? "I have ambition. You should give me a chance."

"I'm sorry Steve. I'm not getting any younger. I have to do what I have to do. Steve, if you don't feel like taking me home I understand."

"No problem. I brought you here. I'll take you back," I say, trying to mask my disappointment.

"Try not to hate me. I needed to be honest."

"Thank you for being honest. You ready to go?"

"Yes. We just need to get some bags for our food."

We leave the mall and I drop Lisa off in front of her apartment building. Lisa tells me goodbye and gives me a kiss on my cheek. She also asks me not to call her again. Damn, she did have nice legs.

****

Tuesday morning and I'm still unemployed. Like that's a surprise. It's not like I've been looking for a job. I still have money from my savings and the unemployment checks won't run out for a while. I know what to do. I'll go downtown to *The Shops*. Not to look for a job though.

Lot of nice-looking women walking through *The Shops*. I've caught a few of them checking me out. They don't look good enough though. What am I going to do with them? Hmmmm, this sunglass shop has a nice looking young lady working behind the counter. She's in there by herself. Time to help myself.

"See anything you like?" The woman asks after I've browsed for a few minutes.

"I'll let you know," I say after looking at the woman. Damn she's fine. She's tall. Maybe an inch shorter than me. She had smooth caramel complexion, with dark eyes, long black hair, and a chiseled, but delicate face. She has a well-proportioned body. Big sexy legs. She blows away any woman that I've seen in a long time.

"Take your time looking. We're not going anywhere," she smiles.

This woman is too fine to play games. "Look my name is Steve. I really don't wear sunglasses. I came here to talk to you."

"I appreciate your honesty. My name is Randi. Pleased to meet you," Randi says as she extends her hand which I take. She has soft hands.

"So do you like working here?" I asked while staring at Randi's face. Man she's beautiful.

"It pays the bills. This is temporary. I'm going back to school to get a master's degree in psychology. Do you work around here?"

"I'm between jobs."

"What type of job are you looking for?"

"I'm looking for a paralegal position."

"That's funny, my former boyfriend is an attorney."

Alright! Former! "Does he like it?"

"He was good at his job. Better at being an attorney than he was at treating me well."

"I can't believe he didn't treat you well."

"Well he didn't. He used me. I would do anything he asked me to do yet it wasn't enough. Towards the end of our relationship he was even fooling around on me. He told me the woman's name."

"That musta been rough."

"It was. It still hurts in fact."

"How long has it been?"

"42 days."

"Counting the days. You must have really loved him."

"I still think about him."

"Who left who?"

"I left him. I had to. There's only so much abuse that I can take."

"He ever come after you."

"That's the thing. He never did. I haven't heard from him since I walked out. That's what hurts the most."

"Is there anything that I can do?"

"I need a friend. I gave so much to him that I didn't make too many other friends."

"I can do that. Tell what. I'll stop down here tomorrow and I'll treat you to lunch. How about that?"

"I would appreciate that."

"It's a date then. I'll see you tomorrow."

"Nice meeting you Steve."

"Nice meeting you too, Randi."

This could be the beginning of a great friendship.

Eight

Man, Randi is cool. She really is good to talk to. I've haven't had a female friend since Jessica. For the longest I would try to have sex with every woman I met. Randi is different though. She's actually fun to be around. Beautiful and good to talk with. Who would have thought? I never thought I would see the day when I could be with a woman this fine and enjoy talking to her. Then again it's hard to have sex with somebody when they're always talking about their ex-boyfriend. Apparently her boyfriend was one of those types who was beautiful on the outside and nasty on the inside. From what Randi told me cuz was making stupid money at a local firm. Cuz had a condo, a Porsche, and a Mercedes. Cuz got paid. That was on the surface though. Cuz was abusive. A control freak. Apparently all he wanted from Randi was somebody beautiful on his arm and somebody to have sex with. Basically he wanted a slave girl. Cuz or Jerome rather, even had Randi move in with him so she could cook and clean for him. He didn't want to marry her though. I guess that might have interfered with him stepping out on her. Jerome wanted so much control over her that he didn't even let her work even though she had a college degree. Some people are a trip.

I had lunch with Randi every day this week. She's very intelligent. She likes to write poetry and stuff. She's thought about writing a novel about her experience with Jerome. She thinks it'll be a best seller. People are a trip. They think there was something so special about their bad relationships that other people will pay to read about them. Whatever. Anyway Randi and I decide to check out a movie. It's called *Masks*. It's about these three people who lead double lives. All of them had a mutual friend who led a double life himself as a serial killer. Who thinks up all these things? It's a good movie though. Randi and I get something to eat afterwards. Just some pizza. Pizza is the perfect after movie meal, especially when you're broke. Now after driving around for a little while we're at the Jefferson Memorial. It's a nice sight at night.

"It's beautiful out here," Randi says as we look out at the tidal basin by the memorial.

"I like the view from here. It's very romantic." It was so nice out here.

Randi reaches over to grab my hand. "Yes it is very romantic."

"Let's check out Jefferson's statue." Randi has the softest eyes.

"Okay Steve."

We walk up to look at Jefferson's statue. We read a few of the quotes and then decide that the view outside is probably better. We walk out and sit on the steps. I sit down first and then Randi sits down on the lower step between my legs. I put my arms around her and kiss her softly on her cheek. She smiles sweetly.

"Thank you Steve that felt good."

"You feel good Randi."

"It's so peaceful out here. I wish I could stay forever."

"It is nice. Maybe we can come back for a picnic during the day."

"That would be so nice Steve. You're the nicest man I have ever met."

"I haven't been called nice in a very long time."

"They probably haven't taken the time to get to know you like I have."

"Thank you then for taking the time to get to know me."

"My pleasure."

"You ready to go then?"

"I would hate for the evening to end."

I stand and help Randi up. "It doesn't have to end." We walk hand in hand to my car.

****

"So this is your apartment? Small but nice. Kind of cozy," Randi says as we enter my apartment.

"Thank you. It's not like the apartment I used to have but it's home. Have a seat on the sofa. Do you want anything to drink?"

"Juice would be all right."

"Coming right up."

I get some fruit juice and pour a couple of glasses. I hand a glass to Randi and sit down next to her. She has a card in her hands.

"A card?" I ask.

"For you," Randi says as she hands me the card. "I took a blank card and wrote something for you."

"Thank you." She has beautiful handwriting. It's a poem.

My Angel

I was sad
I was down
I felt like there was no hope
I was empty
Then one day
I looked up
You were there
My angel

You listened
You understood
You empathized
You cared

You are my shining knight
You are my savior
You are my hero
You are my angel

I love you

Randi

I lean over to kiss her. "I love you too, Randi."

We kiss even harder. About twenty minutes later we pulled out the sofa bed.

****

"Hey sleepy head! Wake up! Breakfast is served." I wake up Randi. Last night was great. It had to be because I'm actually cooking for somebody else. Another thing, I actually told a woman truthfully that I loved her. I can't believe this. Maybe she's the one.

"You cooked for me!?! You're so sweet." Randi gets up and grabs my bathrobe to wear. "What do you have?"

"Sausage and eggs. We have orange juice and toast too. Dig in, there's plenty."

"Steve, you made me feel so good last night," Randi says between bites.

"It felt great being with you."

"I don't want it to end."

"It doesn't have to. What are you doing the rest of the day?"

"Nothing really. I usually relax on Sundays."

"Let's go to the zoo."

"I would like that. You need to take me home first so I can change clothes and brush my teeth."

"I didn't want to say anything." I cover my mouth as if to indicate she has morning breath.

"Listen to you. I should breathe on you," Randi says as she sticks her tongue out at me.

We finish breakfast teasing and playing with each other.

****

I take Randi back to her apartment in Arlington so she could change her clothes. She put on some jeans and a blue T-shirt to match my outfit which was basically the same thing. We then head for the zoo.

After finally finding a parking spot, we walk through the zoo. The zoo is always an interesting place to visit. A lot of interesting sights and then there are the animals. The seals are always a trip. The big cats are always chilling as if they're bored by all the people that look at them. One animal that left an impression was the Black Panther. That was a beautiful animal. Most of the animals would ignore the people. Not the Panther though. Cuz was sitting up and yapping at people. Dag that was a beautiful animal.

After seeing all there was to see at the zoo, Randi and I go for something to eat. We then go back to her place where I read some of her poetry and essays.

"Randi you should try to publish some of this stuff."

"I don't know Steve. This is more for me."

"I know, but maybe you can make some money off of this stuff."

"Maybe. People might not like it. I wrote a lot of about Jerome." Randi reaches into the box to pull out some of her poems. "Here's something I wrote about Jerome when I started to realize there was more to him than met the eye."

"Thanks, let me check it out." I take a couple of the poems and begin reading them. They are deep. All of them have the same theme of light and dark, day and night, yin and yang, good and evil. In one poem she calls him the Harbinger of Hope. The next she calls him the Angel of the Abyss. Damn this is deep.

I hand Randi the poems back. "What made you write these?"

"It was what I was seeing with Jerome. I felt so much power from him. Sometimes it would be good as well as bad."

"You still have feelings for him don't you?"

"Yes... I do... but it doesn't affect my feelings for you."

"What was it about Jerome?"

"Jerome? Imagine a man who literally has it all. Looks, intelligence, charisma. When I met him I didn't see any weaknesses. He was perfect. He was Nietzsche's superman. He willed himself to be better."

"Nietzsche? I read some of his stuff in college. Cuz went crazy towards his later years."

"He did but consider how much influence he had. Nietzsche's philosophy influenced fascism in Italy and then Nazism in Germany."

"I remember reading about that. Nietzsche's superman had a superior will which set him apart from the masses." It's such a turn on to talk to a woman with some real intelligence. I forgot what it was like.

"That was the thing about Jerome. He...was...different. He willed himself to be better than others. I've always been attracted to that type of man. Men who were above the masses. To supermen."

"So you're saying that I'm a superman?" I try not to blush.

Randi gives me a serious look. "Steve, whether or not you think so, you are destined for greatness."

"Me? I'm an ordinary Joe."

"You're more than that. When the time comes you will see that."

"What makes you think this?" She's trying to pump me up.

"I know."

"I really don't know. I don't know what to do. Where I'm going in life. For years I've been drifting. I'm comfortable drifting. I wish other people would see that."

"You know what Steve. I think other people see that you can become something more than what you are now. You're probably not ready right now."

"I know what I'm ready for though." I lean over kiss Randi. I love her.

****

Randi and I spend as much time together in the next few weeks as humanly possible. I still don't have a job. I have enough savings to hold me over along with my unemployment checks. I eat lunch with Randi every day. We always hold hands. Women always look at us and smile. I think I have finally found the one. My soul mate. That was my hope. Something's up though. Randi has been acting strange lately. After dinner and a movie one evening we went back to Randi's apartment. We sit down on her couch. She has a sad look on her face.

"Steve, this isn't going to be easy."

"What is it Randi?" I didn't like the sound of this.

"I have to say it. I've decided to go back to Jerome."

"What!?! Why!?!"

"I'm sorry Steve, I love you. Just in a different way from how I love Jerome."

"He used to abuse you! You left him! You want to go back to him!?!"

"Steve. I know you can't understand. It's just that I...need him."

"You need his money!?! What!?! I don't have enough money for you!?!"

"Steve, it's not about money. I told you about the type of man I'm attracted to. Jerome has such power."

"You said that power was bad! Why are you going back to him!?!"

"I've been talking to Jerome lately. I think he's changed. He told me how much he misses and loves me. I'm sorry Steve but I love him. I have to go back to him. He gave me so much."

"Like I didn't give you anything?! I gave you everything I had! Everything!"

"I'm sorry Steve. I wish it could be otherwise."

"So do I."

"You'll always have a special place in my heart. I hope that we can at least be friends."

"I ...don't know."

"Please don't hate me."

I stand up to leave. "I won't. I can't. Look, take care of yourself."

"Talk to you...later?" Randi has tears in her eyes.

"Maybe." I walk out the door without looking back.

****

I can't believe she dumped me, especially after all that I did for her. I thought we meant more to each other than that. Why does it have to be this way? Forget her. I'm fine. I'll just find another woman. Yeah, that's what I'll do.

Seven

"Anna, what's up?" I ask when Anna she picks up the phone on her end.

"Nothing much." She sounds surprised.

"So what are you doing this weekend?"

"I have plans for this weekend, Steve. Did you have something in mind?"

"I was hoping we could get together. Have some fun like we did last time."

"Sorry dear, I'm going to be spending some time with my kids. Tell you what. When I need some I'll give you a call. I have to go now. I'm on the other line. Talk to you later."

Just like that. She didn't even wait for me to say goodbye. Man this has been one tough week. I still can't believe that Randi dumped me. For somebody SHE had walked out on. After all I had done for her. Haven't been able to do anything this whole week. I've been shamming at the gym. Couldn't concentrate enough to look for a job. Now I'm here on a Friday night with nothing to do. I should...yes the phone. Maybe some woman is going to rescue me from my boredom. "Yo!"

"Steven, I hope that you do not answer the phone like that on a regular basis."

"Mom! How are you! This is a big surprise!"

"You know that I have to check on my little man every now and then."

"Mom I'm twenty-eight and I'm bigger than you. You can't keep calling me your little man."

"You will always be my little man Steven. Even when you are a grandfather."

Sigh. "So what do I owe the pleasure of this call?"

"I'm calling to check on you. Are you all right? Do you need anything? Money? Food?"

She's making me blush. "I'm alright Mom."

"Have you found a job Steven?"

"Not yet. I'm still looking."

"You have been looking for a job for a while now Steven. I read in the paper that the Washington area is saturated with members of the legal profession."

"There are a bunch of lawyers down here. It's alright though. I should be able to find something. All these lawyers need somebody to do their dirty work for them. They'll always need paralegals."

"You do not have to always be a paralegal sweetheart."

"Mom you know I hate when you call me sweetheart."

"Listen sweetheart, you can always go back to school and get an advanced degree. You do not have to always do somebody else's dirty work. You can get somebody else to do your dirty work."

"You sound like one of my friends."

"It is good then that you have sensible friends at least."

"Do you have a point in all this?"

"Do not get short with me young man. I am calling because I am worried about you. You have been drifting for a long time now. Frankly I do not see any good coming. You have to get yourself together. You cannot keep drifting. That is for other people. Not for my son. I had...have higher hopes for you Steven. If I have to, I will come down there and give you a kick in the butt for you to realize those plans."

I try to lighten the mood. "Yes Mom I believe you will. I have enough of your footprints from over the years."

"Apparently I did not plant the shoe far enough."

"You did Mom. Trust me."

"If I did Steven, you would be better off now." Mom sounds sad.

"I'm alright Mom."

"You can say you are all right now Steven but I know better. Any mother would know better."

"I guess."

"Steven, I have to go now. Everybody sends their love. I will talk to you soon. Bye-bye sweetheart."

"Later Mom."

Mothers are a trip. Can't really get mad at them for anything they say to you. They're probably the only ones in the world that have your back.

****

Saturday morning at the gym. What a fun time. Not that many people here so I can concentrate on my workout. Man I'm really cut too! I look good in this mirror. I'm starting to look like one of those models in a fitness magazine. Maybe I can do that for a job. Get paid just for looking good. Sounds alright to me. I know I must look good to this redhead that keeps checking me out. I've seen her several times. Never really said anything to her. She does have a nice body. Pale skin though. Maybe I'll holler at her. Say, here comes Darryl. "What up my brother?"

"Not much bro. How are you doing today?"

"Feeling pretty good. Talked to my Mom last night. She called out of the blue."

"That's what moms are for, to make us feel better," Darryl says distantly.

"I bet your mom made you feel great."

"I wasn't close to my mother."

That's something. "You wasn't? Why not?"

"That's a story for another day. So are you over that young lady that had you down during the week?"

"How did you know I was down because of a woman last week?" Darryl looks at me. "I keep forgetting who I'm talking to sometimes."

"I noticed you weren't as friendly as you usually are. I didn't want to push it at the time.

"Her name was Randi. We met and clicked. Hung tight for a few weeks. Darryl man, she had everything. Beautiful and smart. I mean she actually had some sense."

"What happened?"

"She went back to her ex-boyfriend. After all I did for her."

"Look bro. You can do everything for a person and they will still want somebody else. That's life bro. When it comes down to it, you really didn't know what her needs were. Despite you doing everything for her you still might not have met one of her needs."

"The thing is that her boyfriend was so rotten. She thought he was rotten."

"You have to understand one thing about women. That is that a man can never understand them. Situations like this you have to move on."

"I guess so."

"I know so. Steve I need to get out of here. I'm coaching a soccer game this afternoon."

"Good luck."

Darryl grins. "The other team is going to need the luck. Later bro."

"Talk to you Darryl."

Nothing to do but finish my workout. A few more minutes on the exercise bike and I'll be ready to go.

"Hi," someone says out of the blue.

I look up to see the redhead who has been checking me out these past few weeks. "Oh hi."

"You always work out so hard."

"Trying to lose the pounds."

"You look like you're in great shape."

"Thank you. My name is Steve by the way."

"Jenny, nice to meet you Steve."

"Have you been a member of this gym long?"

"I joined a month ago. I got in town two months ago. I work as an attorney for a firm downtown."

"I'm a paralegal. I'm, as they say, between jobs right now."

"You'll probably find something."

"I definitely will. Are you having fun in D.C.?"

"I haven't really been out. I've hung out with a few friends from college. That's pretty much the extent of my socializing. Otherwise I've been busy with work."

"So what do you have planned for the evening?"

"Nothing. I thought I would stay in and rent some videos."

"Don't do that. Tell you what I'll come get you and we can go hang out at a club," I joke.

"That sounds great."

She took me seriously. "Okay then. We can exchange numbers before I leave. I just have a few more minutes on the bike. Have you been to *Paul's*?"

"Haven't heard of it. Is it a good club?"

"It's a pretty popular club in Adam's Morgan. I think you'll like it."

"It's a date then," Jenny smiles.

****

I pick Jenny up around 9:30. She lives on Wisconsin Ave. near where I used to live. Nice building. Man she looks hot tonight. When I see her in the gym she's usually all sweaty with worn out gym clothes. Tonight she has on a tight top, jeans and cowboy boots. Plus she has her hair done up. We chit chat about this and that on our way to Adams Morgan. After finding a parking spot, we head to *Paul's*.

Once we get to *Paul's*, we get a table and have a few drinks. We make small talk. What strikes me about our conversation so far is how superficial it is. It's like we both know what we really want and this date is just the preliminary. After a couple of drinks we go out on the dance floor. We're really going for it. She can dance. After being out there awhile the DJ plays a slow jam.   Jenny has her arms wrapped around my neck. We're dance cheek to cheek. You would have thought we had been going out for a couple of years. We sit down after the DJ puts on some fast songs.

"You're a good dancer," Jenny says

"So are you. You were wearing me out."

"I hope not. The night is still young. You better save some energy."

"What do you have in mind?"

"I thought we could go back to my place and have a little more private fun."

"You're not having any fun here?"

"Not as much as we could be having at my place."

"I can see your point." Ol' girl musta went through some type of transformation. She didn't seem this aggressive when I saw her around the gym. Then again she did approach me first.

Jenny looks at me and bites her bottom lip. "You want to leave now Steve."

"Yes let's go."

****

Last night at Jenny's was great. She was great in bed. Very attentive. She made it clear though that she didn't want any strings attached. She said that she hadn't been with anybody in a few months and that she was going crazy as a result. This morning I got my stuff and left. I was feeling good for a while until something made me think about Randi. Then I thought about last night with Jenny. It seems like I've had a lot of one-night stands lately. I'm not sure if I'm enjoying them all that much. The sex is good but in all honesty it's getting old. I really enjoyed being with just one woman. I remember when I was younger, I wanted to be with just one woman. I didn't want to chase a whole bunch of women around. I didn't want to be like my father. It's funny how things turned out. If only Jessica had been interested in me the way I was in her. I probably wouldn't be in this predicament now if she was. Ah well, nothing I can do about this now. All I can do is chill.

Six

I finally have a new job. I saw an ad in the newspaper for employment with this litigation support company, WPR. It doesn't pay that much but it's a job. I was really starting to go stir crazy around the spot. The talk shows are really getting stupid. One good thing was that I got to work out more in the gym. My weight is down to 190. I've lost 55 pounds. Maybe I should help other people lose weight. Become a personal trainer or something. Charge $75 dollars an hour. I'm quite sure some sucker will pay that.

This new job isn't that bad. I'm basically looking at some documents and screening them for privilege. Some big court case that I'm not supposed to talk about outside the office. Who cares? My co-workers are interesting. I'm working with three other paralegals. Two white guys and a sister. The funniest is John. Cuz is crazy, with a bit of a gut and is opinionated as hell. He will comment on everything from politics to miniskirts. The other guy is Greg. Greg is tall and lanky. He's one of those real liberal whites. The kind that identifies more with minorities and the "oppressed." He's opinionated too. Greg is an attorney waiting to be licensed in D.C. The last member of this little group is Sheila. Sheila's first love is acting. She's done a little theater and a couple of movies. She's still waiting for her big break. Sheila is very attractive with a well-proportioned body and smooth chocolate complexion. I might have to holler at her. We're sitting around chilling, working, and debating of all things, the discrimination beautiful people face in society.

"I'm telling you guys," Sheila says. "Everybody calls me beautiful and guys are always talking about how good I look, but sometimes it works to my disadvantage."

"I don't see how Sheila," John says. "You must get everything you want. You certainly can't lack for dates."

"But I do. Men will either approach me rudely or not at all. I haven't had a date in a month. I have maybe a few male friends and they're gay."

"So what," I add. "Go to a club with some of your girlfriends."

"Steve, that's the problem. I have one girlfriend and she's married. Women are funny like that. They'll hate somebody they consider more attractive than them."

"I have a cousin who's a model. She says the same thing," Greg says while going through some documents.

"It can happen to men too," John says. "I have a friend from college who looked like a real stud, but all he wanted to do was hit the books. Women would say all sorts of things about him because he would ignore them. Turned out that he was loyal to his high school sweetheart. He ended up getting married to her."

"That's another thing. People make all sorts of assumptions about me because they think that I'm attractive," Sheila says. "They think I'm stuck up, an airhead, a slut, and they haven't had one word of conversation with me."

"That's because most people are jealous of you," I say. "If you think about it and really look around, most people are ugly."

"Oh Steve, everybody is beautiful. Don't think like that," Sheila says.

"Not on the outside Sheila. If everybody was physically attractive these fashion models wouldn't make the bucks they do."

"That's because people are shallow. They're judging a book by its cover."

"I don't know about y'all," John cut in. "Myself, I would rather be a studmuffin. Get all the babes."

We all laugh and go back to work. The pay is bad but at least I have a good time.

****

Lunchtime. One thing good about this job is that it's located in *The Shops*. Easy to walk around since Randi isn't working here anymore. I can eat, and check out the women. Always something to do. A lot of fine women walking around. Speaking of which, who's that over by the elevator? Now she's fine. Her body is anyway. Her face is average. Her body more than makes up for her face. Those legs! Hmmmm, light complexioned, round face, athletic body. She must work out. Nice business suit. She must be some type of executive. Oh man she's getting on the elevator. I'm going to have to catch up with her later. Time to get back to work.

****

"He walked!" Ted yells at the TV.

"You know how it is in the NBA. Everybody gets two steps, NBA superstars get three." Ray says.

Ted looks disgusted. "This is trifling though. How can somebody walk this much and not get called? He must be giving the referees a cut of the huge contract."

I sip some beer. "Hey this is the NBA."

"It's halftime fellas," Ray says.

"This game sucks. Where did they get the referees? CYO? AAU? A rec league?" Ted asks.

"These are supposed to be some of NBA's best referees," I point out.

"As compared to what?"

"Aw Ted leave them alone," Ray says after drinking some beer. "So Steve, how was your first week on the job?"

"It was alright. I'm working with some fools. They're keeping me entertained."

"This is a temp job right?"

"Yeah."

"When are you going get a permanent job? Aren't you tired of temping and making less money than you should be?"

"Yeah I'm tired of temping. I've been looking for a real job. What do you think I've been doing all this time?"

"Honestly," Ted says in a serious tone. "It looks like all you've been doing is sitting on your ass waiting for something to come to you."

"Why you tripping cuz?" I ask.

"Because you're not doing anything with your life. You say you're looking for a "real job" yet you tell us that you sit in your apartment all day watching talk shows," Ray says.

"What else was there to do?"

"For starters you can go out and actually look for a job. It's not going to always come to you," Ted says.

"Ray, Ted. I've put out the resume. I can't force them to give me a call. Besides, WPR isn't that bad."

"Still," Ted says. "It's a temp job. How long are you going to survive on temp jobs?"

"I'll be alright fellas." I shake my head taunting them.

"Steve you need to stop tripping and do something with your life."

"You too Ted? It's bad enough that I gotta catch it from Ray, but now you?"

"Everybody sees that you're wasting your life Steve," Ray says.

"I'm not wasting my life! Why does everybody think that I'm wasting my life!?!"

"Because you are."

"Maybe I am to somebody trying to get a high and mighty MBA," I respond to Ray.

"That MBA will allow me to control my life. Once I have it I won't have to worry about losing my job and my apartment. I won't have to worry about sitting around my apartment watching talk shows and soap operas. I won't have to worry about women dumping me because I'm unemployed or treating me like a hoe."

"Man fuck you!"

Ray stands up. "Don't be cursing in here!"

"Whatever." I stand and point my finger at Ray.

"Get out my place!" Ray yells.

"Fuck both of you! I don't need y'all for jack."

"Steve," Ted says in a surprisingly nasty tone. "Don't come through here again until you do something about your attitude."

"Fine! Later for y'all!" I yell as I walk out door without looking back.

****

Punks. I don't need them anyway. Bamas just jealous. That's all. They see that I'm doing alright and they can't handle that. Forget them. At least I can chill out at the gym today. Darryl isn't around. That's too bad. At least he's cool. I have a couple of other friends at the gym. Even Jenny though I haven't seen her around this past week. She must be busy. Maybe I'll give her a call tonight. Then again maybe I should hit a club and find somebody new. Maybe there's a party going on. Say there's Sean. Now Sean's a wacked brother. Cuz looks straight outta a muscle magazine. I think he's been in a couple of body building competitions. I haven't talked to him that much. I wonder if cuz knows where a party is tonight.

"Yo Sean! What's up cuz?"

"Nothing much," Sean says as walks over to shake my hand.

"Dag man that grip!" I shake my hand out. Sean has a killer grip.

"So what's going on tonight?"

"A friend of mine is having a party near Dupont Circle. There's going to be a lot of fine women there. You want to come?"

"Sure why not. Now the women are going to be fine aren't they?"

"Trust me, you will enjoy yourself."

"You need a ride there?"

"Sure, why not. Here's my number. Give me a call when you're ready to pick me up," Sean said as he wrote his number down on a piece of paper.

"I hope the party is kicking." I take the paper from Sean.

Sean winks. "Trust me, this party will be kicking."

Five

"Yo Sean, What's up?" I ask Sean as he gets into my car in front of his apartment building.

"Nothing much. You ready for this party? The women at this guy's parties are always nice. You can't help but hook up with somebody."

I pull out of the apartment's parking lot. "I hope so. I'll take you at your word."

"I see you working out real hard around the gym. You're looking real cut."

"I'm trying to lose some weight."

"I'm the opposite. I'm trying to gain some weight."

"Cuz you look big enough already. Your chest looks like something that you could sit your drink on. Your arms look like bridge cables. Your traps look like you have two kids up there."

"I'm still small. If I want to compete with the big boys I need to get bigger."

"I can't possibly see how."

"I got big before. I used to be real small."

"You must have been really working out."

"It took more than working out to get this big."

"What did you do?" I already know the answer.

"I started using "juice" a couple of years ago."

"Juice?" I try to sound naive.

Sean looks at me as if I'm stupid. "Steroids man,"

"Isn't that stuff dangerous? I've read about people having all sorts of problems because of that stuff."

"That's if you abuse it. People have all sorts of problems because of overeating donuts. Nobody's complaining about that."

"Still man, is it worth it?"

"Hell yeah! Since I started using juice I've gotten bigger. Women pay attention to me. I've been in several bodybuilding contests. I've even placed in a couple. If I win this contest coming up at the end of the summer I can turn pro and that's where I'll really start making the money."

"Still, the long term effects of the steroids..."

Sean cuts me off. "I'll be all right."

"I hope you're right."

"I am right." Sean is almost belligerent. "We're almost there, you need to find a parking space."

"There should be some spaces around the corner. Hopefully."

****

We find a parking spot after driving around for about ten minutes. After parking we walk about two blocks to the party. The party is given by this brother named Gene, one of Sean's buddies from college. We walk into Gene's basement apartment and see a whole bunch of people standing around and mingling. What was especially interesting about the party was that all the men at the party were Black while all the women were white. The vast majority were Danish in fact. One of the guys explained that these women were primarily nannies. They come over here for a little while to experience the culture and to take care of the kids of rich folks. The guy said that these nannies tend to be wild. Real aggressive too from what I'm seeing. One's been eyeing me since I walked through the door. Dag, now she's coming over here.

"Hello," she says with an accent. She's tall with a shapely body. She can look me in the eye. Her hair is somewhere between brown and blond.

"Yo what's up?"

She leans against the wall mirroring what I'm doing. "My name is Thora."

"I'm Steve. Nice to meet you."

"You look so lonely over here by yourself."

"I'm alright. I've already had a couple of beers."

"This is the first time I've seen you here."

"This is the first time that I've been here. You sound like this party is a regular occurrence."

"Gene has a party every Saturday."

"Dag."

Thora looks me dead in the eye. "You are so cute,"

"You alright too." I'm flattered that Thora thinks I'm cute.

Thora moves closer to me. "Are you from Washington?"

"Me? Naw. I'm from Philadelphia. Where are you from?"

"I'm from Denmark. I work as an Au Pair in Chevy Chase."

"That's cool. How do you like it?"

"It's something to do. The kids get on my nerves sometimes."

"That's a harsh attitude for a nanny."

"It's a way to stay in America."

"Are you enjoying yourself?"

"Yes." Thora leans closer and kisses me.

We kiss for about a minute before we stop and look at each other.

"You're aggressive," I say.

"I see something I want, I go for it. We only go around once."

"I guess I see your point." I grab and kiss her. She slowly put her arms around me and grinds me. We break after about five minutes.

"I know someplace we can go for more privacy," Thora whispers in my ear.

"Where?"

Thora has a mischievous look in her eye. "Right out back. It's dark out there. We'll be all alone. This way."

Thora leads me out of the back door to the garage in the back yard. We go into the garage, close the door and kiss. After a minute she sits me down on this bench. She takes my pants down to around my ankles. Thora gets on her knees and goes down on me. Yeah baby that's the spot.

We go back into the party after twenty minutes. Thora decides that she wants to mingle. Not before she gives me her phone number. After she walk away Sean comes up and gives me a slap on the back.

"Way to go Steve. You've just got a turn with the Freak of the Week."

"What are you talking about?"

"Half the men in this room have been with Thora. I hope you wore a jimmy hat."

"Naw man she just went down on me."

"You probably should have worn a jimmy hat for that too. Thora's a straight up hoe."

"Dag and I thought she wanted me for my sparkling personality."

"Only requirement that Thora has is that you're a man. Hell, somebody told me that she also swings with women."

"I was going to propose to her," I laugh.

****

I spend the rest of the evening drinking. I saw Thora going out back with another brother before the party was over. Ol' girl is working it tonight. I drive home by myself. Sean hooked up with one of the women at the party so he told me he would be alright getting home. I go home and hit the bed. It was an interesting night.

****

I get up about noon. I was asleep a long time. Had to sleep off all that alcohol from the party the night before. After fixing myself some breakfast, I get my stuff and go to the gym. The gym is always fairly empty on Sundays. I basically have the place to myself. I'm going through my usual workout when I see this fine young lady on the stationary bike. She has a killer body. Those biker shorts look good on her. She has a nice chocolate complexion, very smooth. Nice face, she looks like she could be Asian except for her complexion. Being the stud that I am I introduce myself.

"How ya doing, my name is Steve."

"Denise, nice to meet you."

"I've never seen you around the gym before."

"I'm here on a short term membership. I'm from Pittsburgh. I'm doing some work at this law firm downtown."

"Are you an attorney?"

"Yes. What about yourself?"

"I'm a paralegal. I work for a litigation support company."

"Do you like it?"

"It's alright. I'm trying to get a job at a law firm."

"Good luck. There's plenty in DC."

"It's a question of one of them wanting me."

"You look like a competent person."

"Thank you. So do you. So are you enjoying yourself in DC?"

"I've been here for about a week. I'm staying at a hotel downtown. My firm is paying for it. Room service and everything. I haven't been out. Where are some good places to go?"

"DC has a little bit of everything. Clubs, restaurants, museums, you name it, its here."

"I guess I need somebody to show me around."

"Tell you what. How about we go see a movie tonight? *Passed Over* is playing. I heard it's pretty good."

"That sounds like a worthwhile endeavor. I'll give you my hotel and room phone number after I get off the bike. We can decide on what time we're going to meet later on."

"That's a bet. I look forward to this evening."

After some small talk we get back into our workouts. After a little while Denise gives me her information and leaves. She looks good walking away.

****

I pick Denise up later that evening. She looks good in those nice tight jeans and light weight sweater. We make small talk on the way to the movie. Denise graduated college the same year I did. She went to law school after working for a couple of years. She asks if I plan on going to law school. I tell her no and then the most amazing thing happens. She changes the subject. For once somebody wasn't pressing me about going to law school. Denise has a good sense of humor. It's nice to actually have a conversation with a woman. Like I used to have with Randi and back in college with Jessica.

We get to the movie, got the requisite soda and popcorn and sit down to watch the movie. The movie was about a man who is too nice to women. All of them walk all over him. Of course at the end the man ends up with a very beautiful woman who appreciates his niceness. Only in Hollywood. We leave the theater and stop to get something to eat at a pizza place.

"That was a funny movie," Denise says while waiting for our pizza.

"I think all men can relate to cuz in the movie?"

"What makes you say that Steve?"

"Ask any guy, any race, any culture, and he will tell you the same thing. Women don't like nice guys."

"That's not true Steve."

"Then how come bad guys can treat women anyway they want and the women will be all in love with them. Yet these same women will walk right past a nice guy. Then these same women will dog a nice guy if they decide to go out with one."

"Steve, let me explain something. This is something a lot of men should hear. All these women you see clinging to men who are bad for them, who dog them, who keep them down instead of helping them to grow. You know something about these women nice guys don't seem to understand?"

"What?"

"Every single one of these women have low self-esteem. Their view of themselves is so low that they feel that they can't do any better or that worse that they should get dogged. Nice guys are wanted and appreciated by real women, not these little girls out here. Nice guys should just thank God that these women don't want them. These women will only drag a nice guy down."

"You have an interesting way of putting things. You never got dogged before have you?"

"Never, I think too much of myself. Now I have my insecurities like anybody else but I never thought that hanging on to a bad man would help me."

"I think more women need to hear that."

"They know it in their hearts. They know a man can't help them if he doesn't have his own act together. Most women just choose to ignore this fact."

"That's deep."

"Look it like this. How long does a man stay with a woman he knows to be bad for him? Not very long. I mean, she may be able to pull the wool over his eyes for a little while but not for long, especially a man trying to do something with his life."

"You have a point there." This is rare. A woman I can sit and listen to. Very rare indeed.

****

After finishing the pizza, I drop Denise off at her hotel. I ask her if I could come up but she says maybe another time. She gives me a kiss on the cheek and gets out my car. It's funny but that was one of my best dates ever. Despite the fact that I didn't even get a tongue kiss. That's alright though. There's plenty of time for that. The conversation was very nice. It is so nice to talk to an intelligent woman. I think I could fall for Denise.

Four

It's been a rough week at work. They were keeping us busy. If my co-workers weren't there to keep me laughing I might have gone stir crazy. Of course the week was made easier by seeing that babe with the great body walking through *The Shops*. I'm going to have to holler at her one of these days. It's Friday night though, I need to give Denise a call to see what she's doing. I've only been able to talk to her a couple of times this week. I really like her. I told her I would call her tonight to see what she's doing. I'd better call her right now. Hmmm, the phone just keeps ringing. Wait, somebody is picking up.

"*Grand Hyatt.* May I be of assistance?"

"Hello. I was calling for Ms. Denise Anderson. She's in room 723.

"Hold on sir...Sir, Ms. Anderson checked out this morning. Is there anything else I can help you with sir?"

"No thank you," I say as I hang up the phone.

Denise rolled on me. I can't believe she left town without telling me. Man, I finally thought I had met a female with some sense and then she ducks out on me. A man can't catch a break sometimes. I might as well go to the gym now. Nothing else to do.

****

I've been here at the gym for a half hour and I'm still thinking about what Denise did to me. I thought she had more class than that. Man I...

"Hey Steve,"

"What's up Sean? I thought you would be hanging tonight with some fine babe."

"Naw man. I'm in training for this contest coming up in a couple of months."

"A couple of months? You're training so soon?"

"I'm going up against some tough competition. I gotta get started early."

"I guess you know what's best."

"That's right I do. Anyway man I wanted to tell you that I'm leaving D.C. on Sunday. I'm going back up to New Jersey."

"Dag just like that? What about the lease at your apartment?"

"One of my boys is going to take over the lease."

"It seems like I just met you."

"You did just meet me. Don't worry about it though, I'll be in touch," Sean reaches out to shake my hand.

"Yeah man definitely keep in touch." Cuz is one crazy brother.

****

After working out for about an hour it's nice to be home just chilling on the couch watching whatever movie this is on cable. I can't get Denise out of my mind. I still can't believe she rolled on me like that. It seems like every time I meet a woman that I actually like I don't end up being with her. What's wrong with me? I'm not perfect but who is. Just once I want a woman to chill out with. Is that too much to ask? Why can't I get that? Why is it that when I meet someone it doesn't seem like I have enough for them? Then again it's like that for every part of my life. Why can't people just take me as I am and not what they think I should be? Why?

I still can't believe Denise rolled on me without at least saying goodbye. I know we only went out once and talked to each other a couple of times during the week. That should have been enough to warrant at least a good bye. She gave me no indication that she was about to leave so soon. Why couldn't she say goodbye?

Then Sean rolling back to New Jersey. At least he said something. It seems like everybody is rolling on me. I haven't talked to Ray and Ted in weeks. I haven't seen Darryl in a couple of weeks. These women I meet keep rolling. I don't know how much longer I can take this.

****

Wednesday. Hump day. Man am I glad the week is almost over. Not that I have anything to look forward to this weekend. At least there's some fine women walking around *The Shops*. Speaking of fine women, there's that babe I've been seeing around. She's in line to get some pizza. I guess I should hook up some pizza as well. I can't believe I'm this close to her. Her perfume is so sexy. Oh man she's turning around and smiling. She has a pretty smile. I better say something. I can't let this opportunity get away. I break the ice. "That deep dish pepperoni and sausage pizza looks good."

"Sure does. Too good in fact. Could probably eat two or three slices, but I better not. Have to watch my figure," she smiles.

I'll watch your figure for you baby. "You look great. I don't think a couple of pieces of pizza will hurt you."

Her smile gets bigger. "Thanks for the compliment."

"My name is Steve by the way."

"Carol. Nice to meet you. I've seen you around here a lot."

"I work at this litigation support company in this building."

"Are you an attorney or paralegal?"

"Paralegal. Yourself?"

"I work as an attorney with Dowd and Associates. I do mostly criminal work."

She would be an attorney. "You like what you do?"

"I love it. Do you like what you do?"

"Sometimes. Sometimes I think about going to law school." The requisite lie.

"Really, that's interesting. I like a man with ambition."

Where have I heard that before? "That's me, full of ambition."

"How would you like to join me for lunch?"

"I thought you would never ask."

We get a slice of pizza each. Even though I'm broke I pay for her slice and something to drink. After walking around we find a table in the food court. Carol starts talking.

"You say you're interested in law school. That's good. It's nice to see a Black man who's interested in going places. How long have you been out of college?"

"About six years now. I worked as a paralegal at this firm for a long time. Then they downsized about a year ago. I've been working at different litigation support companies since then."

"That must have been tough. I know a couple of people down at the courthouse who were laid off by big firms. It's tough out there for attorneys."

"Not tough enough for me. When I get my law degree, I'm going to get paid." I bob my head a little.

"I like a Black man with a little arrogance."

"You do?" I'm surprised. "Most people seem to think a cocky brother is worst thing in the world."

"It depends on where it's directed. Somebody with arrogance standing out on the street corner doing nothing with his life is stupid. Somebody with arrogance in line to register for classes, a business license, or to pay for a book that will improve himself is smart."

"That's deep."

"Tell me about yourself. Do you have a girlfriend?"

"No. Do you have a boyfriend?"

"No I don't."

"You got down to business."

"I don't like to waste time. I've met too many men who were stupid, lazy, unambitious, ugly, fat, have a criminal record, unemployed. I've met them all. I'm tired. I know what I want and quite frankly you look like you might have what it takes. You're somebody I would like to get to know better."

Heyyy! "I am? What makes you say that?"

"You're obviously ambitious. You're handsome, built, everything I could want in a man. At least initially."

"You sound like you're trying to pick me up"

"Maybe, maybe not."

"Tell you what. Why don't we get to know each other over dinner and a movie?"

"Sounds good to me," Carol smiles.

"Definitely sounds good to me."

Carol and I exchange phone numbers. I walk her to the elevator so she could go back to her office. Man she looks good from the back. I head back to work with a smile. I guess I have something to do this weekend.

Three

"Ummm, the food smells good," Carol says as she sits at her kitchen table watching while I cook her a steak dinner. I'm making New York strip steaks, baked potatoes, broccoli, and rolls. It has been a few days since I met Carol. We talked every night on the phone. I hope she works out. It would be nice if some woman works out. It would have been nice if Jessica had worked out. Damn I'm really reaching back now. I wonder how Jessica is doing now. I wonder if she is still with that knucklehead.

Carol interrupted my thoughts. "Steve, I'll make a salad to go along with the meal."

"That'll be nice. Dinner should be ready in fifteen minutes."

"That will give me enough time to get the salad together." Carol gets up and walks to the refrigerator. She is looking good with a loose green T-shirt and some loose jeans that still managed to show off her phat ass. The sister is definitely built.

Carol reaches into the refrigerator to get tomatoes and stuff for the salad. "You like croutons?"

"That'll be nice."

"How about cheese cubes?"

"Cool.

"How about some ranch dressing?"

"Perfect."

"I like this," Carol smiles. "Making dinner in my kitchen with a handsome man. I love it."

Oh man she thinks I'm handsome. "I love it too. Making dinner in the kitchen of a beautiful woman."

Carol walks over and gives me a peck on the cheek. "You are so special."

"What was that for?"

"For making me feel so good."

"Glad to be of service."

We sit down to eat after I put the food on the table. I open a bottle of Chardonnay.

"This steak is delicious. My compliments to the chef."

"Thank you. Your salad is great. You must have stuck your finger in it."

"Stuck my finger in it?"

"Something my grandfather says. It means that it tastes good because you made it."

"Good response."

Good response? "You said I was special earlier. What makes me special? I'm an ordinary Joe."

"You're more than ordinary. You're intelligent. A lot of men aren't intelligent. You're handsome. A lot of men aren't handsome. You have a nice body. A lot of men definitely don't have that. You're nice, you cook, and you're employed. I think you have a bright future."

"What makes you think that my future is bright?" I'm glad somebody does.

"You're obviously very intelligent. You talk about getting a law degree."

"I don't really think about it that often."

"I think you should. You'll probably be successful." Carol sounds assured. "You've already been in making me happy and that's not easy."

"What do you mean? I'm sure you've experienced happiness in the past."

"We can talk about that after we finish this wonderful dinner."

We finish eating and after putting the dishes away we go into her living room to watch a comedy concert movie, *Patrick Wilson - Live.* The brother is funny. After the movie we have some more wine. Feeling looser Carol talks about her past relationships.

"I really haven't been out with that many men. I guess I've been choosy."

"You have to be. There's a lot of jerks out there."

"I think that I've managed to avoid the jerks, but the guys I did go out with...everything would be fine until they would do something stupid."

"Stupid? Like what?"

"One guy that I had been going out with for five months was late for a date. He didn't call or anything. He shows up to my apartment an hour late and then doesn't explain why he was late. He tried to play it off like nothing happened."

"I don't know why guys are so stupid sometimes."

"I wish you could tell me. There was this one guy I was with who tried to have sex with me without a condom. He said that he didn't have one. When I told him that we couldn't have sex he all of a sudden produced one. I told him to get out of my apartment."

"At least you didn't tolerate his stuff."

"I'm trying to do too much with my life to tolerate any crap. That's what I like about you. You seem like you want something for yourself."

You're about the only one who thinks so. "Thank you. Now let me do something for you. Lay down on the couch."

"What for?"

"I'm going to give you a message."

"Why didn't you say so?"

Carol lays on her stomach. I straddle her and massage her neck. "Does this feel good?"

"Ohh yesss."

Twenty minutes later Carol leads me into her bedroom.

"Last night was great," Carol says as we walk through Beltway Plaza holding hands.

"You were great. You felt so good in my arms."

"I could really fall for you."

"I bet you say that to all the guys."

"Just some."

Carol and I sit down on a bench waiting for the movie theater to open. "So Mr. Walters, have you been out with a lot of women?"

"Yes I have."

"Anyone special."

"All were special in their own way."

"Have you ever been in love?"

"I thought I have been in love but not really." I lie to her. I don't know if I can tell her about Jessica. Damn. It still hurts.

"Really? I know how that feels."

"You do?"

"Yes I do. There was this one guy I didn't mention before. Let's call him Troy."

"Ok, Troy," I mock.

"Very funny."

"I try."

"Anywayyy. Troy was a woman's fantasy. Tall, Cocoa-colored skin, wavy hair, luscious lips, nice buns..."

"Hold up, you're not talking to one of your girlfriends."

"Sorry. You have to understand that Troy was too good to be true. Aside from his looks he was a brilliant college professor. He taught mathematics. It was perfect with him. We could talk about anything. One minute we could be talking about the latest happenings on a soap opera. The next we would be talking about the shift in humanity's mind to a higher state of consciousness."

The what? "Uh-huh."

"It was so perfect. I fell in love with him."

"So what happened?"

"I found out he shared his intellectual insights as well as his body with somebody else."

"Another woman?"

"Worse. Another man."

"Dag, Troy was gay?"

"No he was bisexual. He told me after I confronted him."

"How did you find out?"

"I have a gay friend that I had introduced Troy to. My friend saw Troy with this guy at a club in Dupont Circle."

I grab Carol's hand. "I bet you were devastated."

"I was heartbroken. I thought I had found Mr. Right and he turned out to be a fraud. It's one thing to have to deal with women checking him out, but to worry about men...I couldn't handle it."

"Why a man would want another man after being with you is beyond me."

"Thank you. You always seem to say the right thing."

"My pleasure. Hey, they're starting to let people into the theater. Let's go get a good seat."

Two

Last day on the job. We have finished most of the work for the project. We have a few odds and ends we need to complete. As usual we're chatting about a current issue. Right now we're talking about Black empowerment. As always the conversation is heated.

John is opinionated as ever. "I think Black people need to get off their asses and work. Stop waiting for the government to take care of them,"

"What do you think we've been doing? People won't give us jobs," Sheila says.

"That's right John. We have to do more as a society to empower Black folks. We have an obligation," Greg says. My man Greg, the ultimate liberal. I think he's a member of some socialist group.

"The only obligation we have to Blacks is not to interfere with their progress. We don't have an obligation to help them," John says.

"Yes you do," Sheila responds. "What about the reparations America owes us for slavery?"

"Sheila, I don't think I should have to pay for the crimes of my ancestors. It's unlikely any of them owned slaves."

"Yes, but you are benefitting from what those slaves have built."

"Sheila's right John. The effects of slavery are still apparent in the Black community, especially when you look at the Black family," Greg says.

John looks annoyed. "Don't give me that crap. The Black community was more cohesive closer to slavery than it is now."

"Oh and when did you become an expert on Black history?" Sheila asks.

"I had an African-American studies class in college and I do a lot of reading on my own," John answers.

"Aw, such concern for the brothas and sistas," Sheila mocks.

"I read about all cultures. I'll tell you this much. Every group that has come to this country has pulled themselves up by their bootstraps. The Asians, the Irish, the Italians, the Jews, the Cubans, all of them did what they had to do to succeed."

"None of them were ever slaves," Greg says.

"Blacks may have been slaves but they aren't now. The Civil Rights movement destroyed segregation. Sure there's racism, there will always be racism as long as people are different," John says.

Sheila suddenly turns to me. "What do you think about this Steve?"

"I really haven't thought about this."

"Come on Steve. How can you be Black and not have some type of opinion?" John asks.

"I don't have an opinion. Everything has been alright in my life. I haven't really been affected by racism."

"We've all been affected by racism. Whether we know it or not," Greg says.

"Yeah Steve, you must have something to add," Sheila says.

"Ah leave him alone. How 'bout them Wizards? Anybody see the game last night?" John asks.

We went back to work. Man I hate when people ask my opinion on things. I wish they would let me be sometimes.

Well my little project with the WPR Co. is over. Too bad they didn't have any more work. Now I'm unemployed again. I guess I'll go to the unemployment office on Monday. Man this is bad. At least I still have Carol. I already told her that today would be my last day. Now we can spend more time together, we can...

"Steve, wait up."

Who? Oh it's Sheila. "What's up, Sheila?"

"Steve I wanted to talk to you alone."

"Yeah? For what?" We continue to walk through *The Shops* on the way outside.

"Steve, what was that this morning?"

"What was what?"

"Steve we were having a big discussion on race and you were just sitting there like you were oblivious to everything."

"I don't go for all that racism stuff so I really don't think about it."

"Steve, I can understand that, but I've noticed that you don't seem to take a stand on anything. I've never met a man who doesn't seem passionate about anything. Don't you believe in anything?"

"I...I haven't really thought about it."

"You better. You have too much potential to waste your life. You have to take a stand on something. You have to make a choice."

"Yeah, yeah, whatever."

"Yeah that's right, whatever."

"Why do you care anyway?"

"I care about all of my Black men. I will do anything I can to help my brothers reach their full potential."

"So you're one of those women who believe in supporting their men."

"Only if he believes in supporting himself."

"I'll be alright. I can take care of myself. What are you going to do now? Are you going to get another temp job?"

"Oh I didn't tell you? I'm going to New York to live. I'm going to take some acting classes and audition for some plays. I'm going to take my shot."

"Good for you."

Sheila reaches out and hugs me. "Keep in touch."

"That I will. As long as you acknowledge me after you win the Academy Award."

"I will. You better acknowledge me when you're big and famous."

"Still trying to push me along huh?"

"What else is a sister for?"

****

This is the life. Chilling out at Carol's house. Such a nice place too. I haven't been back to my place since Sunday. Been here a solid week. I'm chilling, drinking beer, watching the talk shows. This one talk show cracks me up. These men said that they were superior to other men because of their high IQ's and their buffed bodies. Give me a break. Anyway I've been sitting around, playing house husband and whatnot. This isn't so bad though. Keep the place straight and make dinner for Carol. I don't know though. Carol seemed cool about everything at first. Lately though she's been acting a little...distant. I'm getting a bad feeling about this. Carol's out in the living room watching T.V. I think I need to see what's wrong. I sit down on the couch. "Carol, you've been kinda distant lately. What's up?"

"I...I might as well get to the point. I don't think that this can go on."

Not again. "W-What do you mean?"

"This relationship."

"Just like that? What's wrong with our relationship? I'm satisfying you right?"

"This has nothing to do with sex. Everything isn't about sex."

"What is this about then?"

"This is about you."

"Me?"

"Yes you. Since you've stopped working all you do is lay around my house."

"I haven't found a job yet. You know that."

"You haven't been looking! Sorry about that. This is getting on my nerves."

"I'm sorry I'm getting on your nerves but it's tough finding a job."

"Not if you try. Steve, I'm trying to do something with my life. I need somebody who's trying to do something with their life. I'm looking for a husband. I don't have time for a "just for the moment" relationship. I need something with some promise.

"You don't see that with me."

"Not anymore"

"So what do you want me to do?"

"I want you to get your stuff and leave."

"Just like that? Are we going to be friends at least?"

"I don't think so."

Just like that it's over.

****

She dumped me. Like they all do. Why? What the hell do I have to do? Here I am laying in my bed, in my apartment that I haven't been in for a week, alone. I always end up alone. Why? What the hell do I have to do to be happy? Why is it always like this? Why!?! Damn, I'm crying. Why is it always like this? Where has my life gone this past year or so? I had a job getting paid big money, I lose it. Had friends. They're not even speaking to me. How did I get to this point? How!?! I thought I was a ladies' man but they keep dumping me like an unwanted whore. They use me and then leave me. Why!?! Now Carol. I thought she would be the one. Hell I thought all of them would be the one. Now I have none of them. Why is this happening to me? What did I do wrong? What kind of future do I have? No job. In fact the prospects have never been worse. Absolutely nothing to look forward to. Where can I go? What can I do? Is it even worth living anymore? Is anything worth it? Damn, I'm crying more now. Is this what I've come to? I'm lying here with no future and no friends. I don't know what to do.

One

God help me. I've hit the bottom. I'm at zero. Please help. Show me the way.

BOOK II

ZERO

Reflection

I have been laying here for three days. I haven't gone out. Haven't got any calls. Haven't done anything. How did my life get to this point? Everything seemed to start alright. I remember when I was a kid. I had a big house, nice neighborhood in West Philadelphia, plenty of friends. I remember how proud I was when my father and mother would visit my school. Everybody, even the teachers, seemed to be impressed with my father, Dr. Jeremy Walters, big, strong, and handsome. He had everybody thinking he was so great. I thought so too at the time. It was years later that I realized he wasn't such a great dad. He was very stern, always pushing me to be better, to achieve more. I guess it helped in a way. I did get the best grades. Everybody thought I was the smartest kid in school. That wasn't bad considering that it was an

Rom Wills

exclusive private school with lots of bright kids. What was my IQ?
120 or something like that. Whatever it was, my father wanted to
make sure I lived up to my potential. Funny, he was not as hard on
my brother and sister.

My mother, Mary Walters, Ph.D., was, is, a strong woman.
I forget how many degrees she has but I guess what made her
strong was how she showed her love for the family. I guess she
really showed her strength by staying with my father despite his
numerous affairs. Everything was about the family with my
mother. She always put the family first. No matter how many
classes she taught, no matter how many organizations she belonged
to, she always made her family her top priority. She took the edge
off of some of my father's sternness. Mothers will always have
their children's back. Then again she always wanted me to do my
best. To reach my full potential. God how did I reach the point
I'm at now?

God. I remember that I had a strong faith in God. Where
did that go? I remember I used to love going to church. Listening
to the choir. Participating in Church activities. The best thing I
miss about church was listening to Reverend James. Reverend
James used to teach more so than preach. I remember every month
he would have the kids come up to the front and listen to a special
sermon. One sermon stood out more than others. It was when I
was twelve. He called the kids to the front. I brought my little
brother with me. My sister stayed with our parents. Reverend
James talked about Luke 12:48. He said, *"Much is required from the
person to whom much is given. Think about it my children. You are so blessed
to be here. You are so beautiful and well-behaved. You are so smart. You*

bring great joy to your parents." I remember looking out into the congregation seeing my mother and father smiling broadly. It was one of the few times I recall seeing my father smile.

Reverend James continued, *"My children, you have been given so much. You must share your gifts for that is God's word. Little Kathy, an angel whose voice fills the building. You make us all feel so warm. You must share that gift with the world. So that all can feel good. Little Phil, always reading the bible, always quoting the scripture. Even standing up in front of the church big and tall and correcting me during the middle of my sermon."* The congregation broke out laughing then.

Reverend James pointed out the gifts and talents of each and every child up there. Then he got to me. He said, *"Steven, you are so brilliant. You can be so many things. A doctor like your father. A professor like your mother. A lawyer, an architect, anything you want to be. But no matter what you do...you must give back. You must not use your talents for selfish gains. You must use your gifts for the good of all, Steven and all of you. That is the meaning of Luke 12:48. That is why Jesus gave his life so that we may be saved from our sins. That is the word of God."*

I'll never forget what Rev. James said yet somehow I haven't practiced what he said. I did at first though. In high school I played sports though I wasn't the greatest athlete. Funny, I was still team captain in football even though I didn't start. Coach said it was because I was always encouraging others. Seemed like I brought out the best in others and also because I had the best grades on the team. I was always helping others. Volunteering at soup kitchens all the time. Volunteering at children's homes. President of the student council two years straight. Honor roll so many times the teachers joked about naming it after me. Class

Valedictorian. Over one hundred colleges wanted me to come to their schools. Ended up going to St. James. Not too far from home. Guess I didn't want to go too far from my mother's cooking. St. James offered me a full ride. That's funny because after talking with my parents I decided to turn down the scholarship. Told them to give it to somebody less fortunate. My parents were proud of me. They had no problem paying for tuition. Even more they paid for me to live on campus. I still remember how my mother was grinning mischievously while saying she couldn't wait to get my brother and sister out of the house.

I was off to college. What an experience.
Challenging classes.
Stimulating professors.
Dorm life.
Parties.
All-nighters.
Ballgames.
Intramurals.
Jessica.
Damn.

Jessica Barnes. Damn, she was fine. Met her on the first day. She was from D.C. Finished on top of her class at a prestigious private school. Politics major, same as myself. She was light brown with green eyes and brown wavy hair. She had played sports in high school as well as danced since she was five. She had brains, beauty, and a body. She was perfect.

I fell in love.

As fine as she was I didn't fall for her right away. It was all about intellectual stimulation. I could talk to her. This was the first time I could relate to a woman intellectually. I had been out with a couple of girls before though they were just high school flings. Nothing serious. Jessica though, she was something. We could talk about politics, the environment, the latest movies, the stupidest T.V. shows, we could talk about anything. I saw her as a friend until one night I saw her differently. I wanted to be with her in a different way. I was going to tell her how I felt. I remember going to her room to talk with her about my feelings. I thought it would be the beginning of something special.

How wrong I was.

I got to her room and she hugged me and told me that she had something to tell me that I couldn't tell anybody else. I was like, *"What's up?"*

Jessica said, *"Steve, you can't tell anybody else, I'm not a virgin anymore."*

Oh.

Jessica continued, *"I had sex with Chris Johnson. He was my first. It felt so good."*

"I...it did?"

"Yesss!"

"Jessica, doesn't he have a girlfriend at another school?"

"Yeah but he said he is going to leave her."

"You believe him?"

"Yes."

"Why?"

"Because I'm in love with him and he's in love with me."

"He said that!?! How do you know he's sincere?"

"Because it feels right. I'm so happy. Please be happy for me too."

"I am," I remember saying to her. Lying through my teeth.

Chris ended up breaking Jessica's heart. After having sex with her a few more times he decided to move on to greener pastures. Jessica cried on my shoulders all night after Chris dumped her. I still loved her. I wanted to tell her right then but I felt the time wasn't right.

After a week, Jessica started hanging out with this football player. Now he dogged her. His own boys tried to warn her to stay away from him. She didn't listen. She thought she was in love. When he dumped her, she cried on my shoulder again. Again I didn't tell her how I felt.

Jessica went out with two other guys our freshman year. Again she thought she was in love. Again she would get dumped. Again she would cry on my shoulders.

Again I didn't tell her how I felt.

I felt like she would reject me.

I didn't feel like I was her type.

The men she went out with were dogs.

I wasn't a dog.

They cared for nothing but themselves.

I still volunteered at soup kitchens.

They did nothing for the community.

I made the Dean's List as a freshman.

They barely studied.

I stayed out of trouble.

One of them had been barred from living on campus.

I mean I didn't totally wait for her. I had a meaningless fling or two. Jessica was the only one I really wanted to be with.

The whole pattern kept up as long as we were there. Then as we were getting close to Christmas of our senior year Jessica fell in love again.

The brother's name was Devon. Jessica said she met him walking down the street in Center City. Devon didn't have a job, any ambition, was selfish, barely got out of high school, he wasn't even particularly good looking. Even some of Jessica's friends wondered what was up. Jessica didn't care. So much so that she left school in March because he was worried that she might have left him because she would have had a college degree.

I remember the day she left she was like, "*Please be happy for me. I have to do this.*"

"*Why are you throwing your life away?*" I asked.

"*I'm not throwing my life away. For the first time, I'm truly happy. We love each other. I know he isn't much in most people's eyes but we're happy with each other. I'm happy. I can't say it enough. Please be happy for me Steve. I love you,*" Jessica said as she embraced me.

"*I love you too,*" I responded.

"*I know. I've always known but I never thought about you in a romantic way.*"

"*I didn't know how to tell you.*"

"It wouldn't have mattered."

"Oh."

"Bye Steve."

Like that she was gone.

She knew.

She knew how I felt.

She knew how I felt and it didn't matter.

She chose somebody who was the opposite of me.

I was trying to make something out of my life. I always strived to do my best. To be of service to others. To reach my potential.

It didn't matter.

It just didn't matter.

If the woman I loved despite everything didn't want me what was the point of trying to do my best?

What was the point?

I had wanted to go to law school. Be a lawyer. Help people. Reach my potential. What was the point of reaching my potential if there would be nobody to share it with? How could things be this way? Why is God doing this to me? Why didn't God do something?

I remember clearly now. That was when I changed. I decided that trying to achieve something is a waste. Having ambition is a waste when the women will just go for the guys with no ambition anyway. That's what I thought then. Now with these women rejecting me because of a lack of ambition I don't know.

I turned my back on God back then.

I was so hurt by Jessica's rejection.

I wondered how God could let me feel this much pain.
Now I'm not so sure I did the right thing.
God I need you back in my life.

The Choice

I have been in bed for a couple of weeks. I don't feel like doing anything. Haven't been exercising. I've been laying here crying about how messed up my life is. Look at me crying like a baby. Smelling like hell. Haven't showered since leaving Carol's My hair and face are all scraggly and I'm so tired. Maybe I should end it all. No, I'd probably mess that up too.

Sleepy as hell.

Drifting off.

God help me...please help me...please God help me...me please...

"More is required from those to whom much is given. Much more is required of those who much more is given," says Reverend James.

Reverend James? Where am I? I'm in church but I'm an adult. What's going on? Everything is so crazy.

What the hell is this?

Wait.

Where am I now?

Wait, I know where I am...Jo's apartment.

"We all have to help each other," Jo says.

But who's helping me?

"You need to do something with your life," Ray says.

I am in Ray and Ted's apartment. I haven't spoken to them in a long while. Kinda miss them.

Why are you two always on my case to do something with my life? What does it look like I've been doing?

"Honestly," Ted responds. "It looks like to us all you have been doing is sitting on your ass waiting for something to come to you."

What do you want?

"You're an intelligent brother," Joe says. We're sitting in his office back at the firm. *"Why are you wasting your life? You're intelligent enough to be whatever you want to be. You have talent. There's a passage in the Bible which basically says that if you're given a certain talent you have an obligation to use that talent for the good of others. You're supposed to multiply that talent."*

"That is the word of God," Rev. James says.

I'm floating.

Drifting.

I'm not going forward.

I'm not going backwards.

I'm going nowhere.

"You don't seem like you're trying to get anywhere in life," Tamara *says as I sit frustrated in her living room.*

I don't know where to go. How to get there.

"You need to work on your attitude," Samuel *says at the expo.*

"I want a man who has some ambition," Lisa *says at the food court.*

What do you want?!

Do I have bad attitude?!

Do I lack ambition?!

Face the truth no matter how harsh it may be," Stephanie *says at the office.*

Maybe I do have an attitude.

Maybe I do lack ambition.

Maybe I'm nothing.

"Whether or not you think so, you are destined for greatness," Randi *says.*

Am I?

I can't find a job.

Don't know where I'm going.

God show me the way.

Why won't you show me the way?

"When God needs you he'll find you," Dwayne *tells me in the office.*

God has forgotten about me.

"I see why you have fallen so far," my father *says in my apartment.*

What do I do?

Where do I go?

I've drifted for so long.

I don't where to go.

What to do?

How do I stop drifting?

God tell me what to do.

You don't seem to take a stand on anything," Sheila says as we walk *through The Shops. "I've never seen a man who doesn't seem passionate about anything. You have too much potential to waste your life. You have to take a stand on something. You have to make a choice."*

Take a stand?

Make a choice?

What do I stand for?

Where do I begin?

I don't know what to do.

Where do I start?

"Start from zero," Darryl says calmly.

Start from zero?

Just like that?

I...don't know.

Should I bother?

Choose.

Choose what?

Greatness.

Mediocrity.

Do I help others?

Do I be selfish?

Choose.

Wait where am I?

I'm in darkness.

I'm alone.

No. I hear people speaking.

Choose.

I don't know what to choose.

I'm in so much pain.

When I gave...I was hurt.

My heart was broken.

I was happy when I kept to myself.

Wasn't I?

Choose.

I don't know what to choose!

You can choose anything you want Steve.

Who are you?

Forgot about me already. I'm sad.

Jessica?

Hi Steve. Long time no see.

I haven't seen you since college.

I know.

Where have you been? I think about you a lot. Where are you now?

Now...Well let's just say I'm happy now.

Are you still with Devon?

No.

Who're you with then?

I'm with a very special man but this is not about me. Steve, you have to make a choice. It has to be to be the right choice.

How will I know what the right choice is?

You will know. When the time comes you will know. Don't make the same choices that I made. Starting with Chris I made all the wrong choices. Devon was the worst. Because of that choice I got into drugs, homelessness, even prostitution. I went low. Real low. Then it was over.

What happened?

Like I said, a special man came into the picture.

Who is he?

You'll see. Steve, this isn't about me. It's about you. You've been blessed with many gifts but you're not using them. I remember how kind you were with me. No matter what I did you believed in me. You never gave up on me. You showed a special kind of love. You need to show that love towards others. You have so much power that you have to release it. If you don't you'll destroy yourself. You have to make a choice. Bye Steve, I'll always love you.

I'll always love you.

Choose.

I want to choose.

I don't know what to do.

I have to do something.

Whatever I do I have to...

Rom Wills

Start from zero.

I awaken in a sweat.

Time to get started.

BOOK III

ASCENSION

One

Monday morning. What a weird dream I had last night. "Start from zero," huh? I guess that's what I should do. What I should do first is clean up. Clean up. I need to clean up a lot. Myself, this apartment, my life. Ah well let me start with myself. First let me take a look in the bathroom mirror.

Damn!

I look like hell. Homeless people would look at me and give me their spare change.

Look at my hair and face.

Woo, my breath. I guess that's what happens when you don't brush your teeth for a while.

First thing I better do is brush my teeth.

Ah yeah that feels better.

Let me take a shower. Turn on the water. Ahhh, too hot on my hand. Ah now it's too cold. Ah just right. Time to get in.

Ummm that feels good. I'll take my time. Wash all this dirt off. All the dirt from the last year or so. I gotta cleanse myself of everything. I have to change. It'll probably take a while. Change doesn't happen overnight. I have to take it one step at a time.

Ahhh the shower did a brother good! Gotta do something with my hair. This scraggly beard too. Let's see. I'll get my clippers. Maybe I'll cut my beard into a goatee and my hair into a fade. Naw I won't do that. I need a symbol that I'm starting from zero. I know the perfect haircut for that.

Yeah boy that looks good. I've never had a bald head before. Not bad. I wonder what women will think about me now. Women. That's how I got into trouble to begin with. I need to chill out with women. Well maybe not totally. I do need to find Ms. Right. Or should I say, Mrs. Walters. I'll find her, I know I will and she'll be my best friend. Now I need to get some clothes on and clean up around here.

That was a chore. I didn't know that this place got so dirty. It's clean now though. Took all day. I'm not really tired though. I guess that since I've been in bed for so long I have a lot of energy. I need to work out. Where did I put my gym bag? Oh here it is. I'd better go to the gym. Maybe I'll see Darryl or Ray. I haven't hollered at them in a long time. Ah well, one step at a time. I'd better get out of here.

Hmmm, I have a new neighbor. Movers are moving somebody into the one-bedroom next door. Can't be these big ugly greasy men. Hope not. I hope it's that young lady holding those clothes. Now she's fine. She has a model's body. Not as slim as those supermodels, but she's nice. Hair combed into a ball. Cocoa-colored skin, almond-shaped eyes. I'm going to have to introduce myself later. Now I need to get myself to the gym.

****

These weights are killing me! Feels like a good death though. My body needed it though. Now to just chill out on the exercise bike. Hmmm, now there's a familiar face. "Yo Darryl! What's up man?"

"Well look who we have here," Darryl responds. "The dead have come back to life. The phoenix has risen from the ashes. Apparently ready for a new direction in life."

"What makes you say that?"

"I can tell from your shaved head. When our African ancestors went into battle, several of them would shave their heads. Particularly warriors of the Nuba tribe."

"Really?"

"That's right. A man shaving his hair off always symbolizes a new beginning. That's why military recruits get their heads shaved."

"As always you're right. I've been going down a bad path. Now I want to go in the right direction."

"Good for you sir. Do you know exactly where you want to go?"

"Not really. I've been stuck in the same place for so long that I don't know."

"Well look at it like this bro. Few people know where they want to go in life. It's like going on the highway. Sometimes you have to get on the road and drive. Don't stay in the same place. You have to keep going no matter what. Along the way, you'll discover your destination."

"That's deep man."

Darryl smiles. "Yeah I know."

"I guess I have to get started."

"That you do bro. Always remember this. As long as you're going in the right direction, others will help you along. Watch, you'll see."

"I believe you. Like I always say, you're a wise brother."

"And like I always say, I wasn't always "wise" as you call it. I'll tell you about it later. Have a nice workout bro."

"Later Darryl."

****

Oh man that was a nice workout. Now I'm back at the spot. Let me just get my key out. I was hoping to see my new neighbor but I guess that will have to wait for another opportunity. That's alright though.

Hello apartment. I'm back. Hmmm, I got a message. For the first time in a while. I wonder who called.

Beep. "Hello Steve, this is Judith from human resources at WPR. I was wondering if you could come in to work on a coding project that will begin Wednesday. Please give me a call as soon as possible." *Beep.*

Coding? Coding? I don't want to code. That's for morons. I'm not going to call them. Wait. What am I saying? It's a job. Not the one I wanted but it's a job. I'll give them a call tomorrow morning. I guess I really am starting from zero.

Two

Well that takes care of that. I start work Wednesday morning. At least I don't have to worry about how to dress going to work. All the coders I have ever seen come to work dressed like whatever. I'll wear some polo shirts, jeans, and some high top basketball shoes to top it off. Yeah, that'll do the trick. At least until I get another job. One step at a time though. At least coding is not too difficult. Anybody can do it.

Ah man. Now I have nothing to do but sit back and chill. Funny, this time a month ago I would have been watching a talk show or a soap opera. I don't feel like doing that anymore. It was such a waste. Other than laughing the only thing I learned from them is that generally stupid people have no problem sharing their stupidity with the world, but that's entertainment. What can you do? I need something to stimulate me. I just realized something. I don't read like I used to. I remember I used to read everything I got my hands on. Now I don't even get a newspaper. First thing I need to do is call for a newspaper subscription. Start reading the paper all the way through. I should start picking up some national news magazines. Yeah I'll do that. Maybe I should go back to school. I don't know what I should do. I know I don't want to practice law. The things I liked most were politics and history. Maybe I should get some books on African history. That was interesting what Darryl said about African warriors shaving their heads before going into battle. I need to find out more about that. Amazing, I'm actually curious about something. I haven't been curious about anything since college. Amazing what hitting bottom can do for a man's thinking. I need to go out for a little, walk around maybe. Go to the park, chill out, take in nature, such as it is in the middle of the city. Then I need to take care of something this evening.

****

I should have done this a while ago. I hope the bamas are home. Come on fellas I know you are here.

"Well look whose back," Ted says as he opens the door to the apartment and extends his hand. "Coming here looking like a bowling ball."

"Couldn't resist could you?" I enter the apartment shaking Ted's hand.

"Let me guess. You got a job at a bowling alley. You've been knocking down a lot of pins."

"Naw man."

"Hey Ray! The prodigal son is back and he got a big, bald, round head! Put on your shades! His head is shining!"

"Hey fool." Ray says as he walks out of his bedroom in his usual non-chalant manner.

"Just chilling," I answer.

Ray shakes my hand. "That's my line."

"Fellas, I came by to say that I'm sorry for my behavior a while ago. I was just stressing over different things."

"You don't have to apologize. We know that you're a stupid knucklehead anyway," Ray says.

"Yeah only reason we let you come around is that you have a car. Couldn't stand you otherwise. Now we can use your head for a basketball. Damn you got a big round head," Ted says.

Good, they're not mad at me. "So what have y'all been doing since I was through here last time?" I sit down on the easy chair.

"I got a promotion on my job," Ted says. "Sales have been going well. I'm now an assistant manager for the Atlantic region. I guess more people want insurance. I am disappointed though."

"Why?" I ask.

"I expected to be president by now," Ted says.

"What about you Ray?" I ask.

"Me? I'll get my MBA in May and then start on an executive track with The Durant Company."

"The Durant Company!?! That's one of the top companies in the nation. You seem as excited about it as you would about changing the channel." I'm always amazed at Ray's non-chalant manner.

"Come on Steve. You know how Ray is. He could get five bullets pumped into him and his reaction would be, "I guess I should go to the hospital," Ted says.

"What's to get excited about? I knew I was going to graduate and I had to get a job somewhere," Ray says calmly.

"You two are a trip. The comedian and the laid-back brother," I say.

"Now that you're back," Ted says. "We have a bowling ball."

"You're not going to let it go are you Ted?" I ask.

"No."

"So what are going to do for yourself Steve?" Ray asks.

"Honestly, I don't know. I do know I'm going to do something. I just don't know what."

"That's a step in the right direction," Ray says. "We'll have our feet in your back until you get there."

"Thanks man."

"What else are brothers for?"

"Hey Ted. You've been quiet for a few minutes. What's wrong?" I ask.

"Just..." Ted says. "Just looking at your big-ass head. You got a big head. A big, brown head. A big, brown, bald, head. A big, brown, bald, ugly..."

It's always good to be among friends.

Three

Well got past the first day morning on the job. Not bad. Not good, but not bad either. Coding seems easy enough. All we have to do is pick up some information from some legal documents and enter it into a computer database. Simple stuff. I have some interesting co-workers. My supervisor is this brother named Fred. Cuz is about 50ish with light-brown skin and wavy hair. Cuz is back in his office chilling. I have a few dozen co-workers, two of them stand out. One's this light-skinned, plain-looking, gap-toothed brother named Dave. He's a trip, into everything. Not only is he working here but he has a part-time job doing market-surveys in a shopping mall. It also seems like he has about a hundred business schemes. He seems like he has a lot of energy for someone who looks like I did when I was 240.

The other co-worker that stands out is this sister named Gloria. Small brown skinned sister with big expressive brown eyes and prominent cheekbones. She has long black locs which she wears in a ponytail. I would ask her out except for the fact that she has a big wedding ring on her finger. She's cool to talk to anyway. She seems really calm and sure of herself. She mentioned that she has just moved into the Washington area and her husband is an attorney with the Department of Justice. She hasn't had time to find a steadier job yet. This project is supposed to be temporary. So they say. I overheard somebody saying that they may keep people for another project. I plan to be one of those people if that is the case. I don't think I can handle unemployment again.

"Hey Steve, you awake?" Dave asks, bringing me back to the world.

I start typing in information. "Yeah man, I'm awake. It's just that this stuff is so tedious it's hard to stay focused"

"It's tedious, the money's all right though. I'm trying to make as much as I can and learn as much as I can. I might start a litigation support company one day. The more I know the better."

"You really think that you can use this stuff? Coding doesn't seem like it's something to make money on."

"The government and several big companies pay a lot to have this done for them. It might seem small and mindless but it's important to somebody."

"Yeah but it's not important to me. It's something to do until something better comes along."

"Hey that's how I look at it too but I might as well learn something while I'm here."

"You two need to stop," Gloria interrupts. "You two should be quiet and do the best job you can while you're here.

Neither one of you would be here if you had other jobs so be happy you have one and give your best effort."

"You have a point Ms. Gloria," Dave tells her.

"I don't know, it's so boring," I say.

"It's your first day dear. Take your time going through and you'll probably find some interesting things," Gloria points out.

"I know that's right," Dave says. "I know I'll find something that I can use in business."

"You and business," I say. "Since I met you this morning you've started ten businesses."

"You know what? Before we leave work this evening I will probably start ten more."

****

Yeah first day at work was a trip. I have an interesting crew this time around. Dave is always coming up with business ideas. I hope he makes it. He might be able to give me job. Gloria on the other hand is such a calm sister. She impresses me as the type of woman who is good at Irish diplomacy. She could tell you to go to hell in such a way as to make you look forward to the trip. It's funny, but as tedious as this job is I feel like I'm going to get a lot from it and especially the people.

Four

Been on this job for three weeks now. I'm still bored silly. I did have some fun away from the job when I hung out with the fellas for my birthday. I'm now the big two-nine. Man I'm getting old. This job is still driving me crazy. I'm daydreaming on the job as much as I have been before. I don't know. I'm trying to go forward but I wonder if I'm going anywhere. Ah well I'll keep plugging away. Gloria is getting into this stuff though. In fact she seems to really enjoy this. Tedious at it is. She's been doing quality control lately. Usually if the work is bad enough she would return it to the coder. She's isn't supposed to spend too much time on someone's work. We all have to produce a certain number of coded documents every day. Gloria though has spent a lot of time on one person's work.

"Hey Gloria, you've been working on somebody's documents for a long time."

"This...person didn't pick up a lot of information."

"Well you're not supposed to do their job for them."

"I don't mind."

"Gloria that could affect your stats. That could affect your job."

"Steve I have to do this."

"Why?"

"Because this is your work."

****

Gloria wanted to talk with me outside the building. I still can't believe she went through all that trouble for me. Here she comes now. "Hi Gloria."

"Hey Steve."

"I appreciate what you did."

"Thank you but I'm not doing it again."

"You won't have to."

"You sure Steve? I heard from some of the other Q'Cers that your work isn't up to par."

"I haven't got anything back though."

"That's because you do well enough to get by. What I had today was really bad. I did it over."

"Why would you do that for me?"

"Because I care about you and I believe you should help the people you care about."

"You care about me enough to jeopardize your own job?

"Christ said a man can show no greater love than to lay down your life for your brother. Even though we've known each other for such a brief time you feel like a brother to me. I'll do anything for my brother."

"Thanks."

"Steve I see a lot of potential in you. I see that you want to go in the right direction. I want to help in as many ways as possible, but I'm not doing your work for you anymore."

"I understand. I'll get my act together. Anything I can do for you? Buy you lunch or something?"

"You have to do two things to pay me back," Gloria smiles. "First I have to be able to go through your work without finding any mistakes. Okay maybe an 'occasional' mistake. Secondly, somebody will need your help in the future. You must give that help, sincerely and unselfishly."

"I promise to do my best. Thank you again."

Gloria nods. "That's what sisters are for?"

****

Saturday night. It's been good week at work. Gloria told me that my work has improved greatly. I was glad to hear that. I need to improve for myself and I didn't want to let her down. In fact since I'm trying harder, I'm enjoying myself more and learning a lot about bank fraud. I remember when Darryl told me that I should learn something from every experience. Darryl's a wise brother. I wonder about his background. He keeps hinting that it was interesting. Maybe I'll find out one day.

Saturday night. Party at Ray and Ted's. Parties at their place are always interesting. I remember their last party. They took their beds up in their rooms for more space and then they set up something different in each room. Last time they had the T.V. in Ted's room set up to play music videos. Ray's room was set up for dancing. The living room had the food and chairs where people could sit around and mingle. The fellas said that they were going to set up like that again. I need to get over there.

****

"What's up Ted," I say as I walk through the apartment door.

"You're late man."

"Late? It's 9:30. I thought I was early."

"You know how it is when we give something. You have to get here early or the food is gone. You know Ray can cook his ass off. Why do you think I stay here? It's for the food. When he gets married the woman's not going to want him for money or sex. She's going to want him for a well-cooked meal."

Ray walks up with a beer in his hands. "And I thought you were here 'cause we're boyz."

"Sorry to inform you... I'm here for your broiled chicken," Ted says.

"You brothers are a trip. Where's the food?" I ask.

Ray points to the dining room. "Over there."

Hmmm. What a spread. Chicken wings, these little egg things, celery and dip, not bad. Big ass brother over here with a plate of food.

"What up man." I reach for a plate to get some food.

"Grubbing," the brother responds between bites. Cuz is big. About 6'5" 300 pounds. Cuz probably works in a warehouse or something.

"Food good?"

Cuz is munching like crazy. "Yeah."

"My name is Steve by the way."

"Phil," Cuz says half-oblivious to me.

"Do you know Ray and Ted?"

"I know Ray."

"How do you know Ray?" Ray didn't seem like the type to know a lot of blue collar types.

"We go to the same school."

"You're in college?" I'm surprised. Phil didn't seem like the college type.

"Actually," Phil says while looking me in the eye for the first time. "I'm finishing up my Ph.D. in African-American studies. I'm doing my dissertation on Denmark Vessey and his attempted slave revolt in 1822. It's a fascinating chapter in history that doesn't receive the attention it should in contemporary history books."

"I remember reading about Vessey in high school. There may have been a paragraph or two. All I got from it was that he planned a revolt that was stopped before it could get started." I try to hide my shame in judging Phil by his outward appearance.

"Naw brotha. It was way more complex than that. Vessey had created a cell-like organization to carry out the revolt. The average slave only knew who his cell leader was and his specific objective. Only Vessey and his lieutenants knew the whole plan."

"That's something. I want to read more about Black history. Not just here but throughout the world."

"I can hook you up with some books. I have books you cannot find in most bookstores. Catch me before you leave or get my number from Ray."

"All right. Thanks man." Man it seems like people are coming out of the woodwork to help me with something. Darryl was right.

Party hasn't been bad. A lot of positive people here, especially that young lady who came in a little while ago. She looks nice. Nice brown delicate face, haircut to her neck. Pretty brown eyes. Very expressive. Nice shapely body. I better holler at her. I approach the young lady with my hand extended. "Hello. My name is Steve."

She softly shakes my hand. "My name is Carlita,"

"Are you enjoying yourself?"

"Yes I am, especially now."

"So do you know Ray and Ted?"

"No, I'm here with a girlfriend. She works with Ted."

"So what do you do for yourself?"

"I work as a sales person for a clothing store in P.G. Plaza. What do you do?"

"I work as a paralegal for WPR Company."

"That must be exciting. You must have been to college to job like that. I'm impressed."

"Well I didn't go to college to become a paralegal. I just ended up as one."

"I'm still impressed that you went to college. I wish I could have went earlier. I'm going to start taking some community college classes next year."

"Good for you. We all have to strive to do better in life." Those words are coming out of my mouth?

"So do you have a girlfriend?"

"No. Do you have a boyfriend?"

"No but I like tall muscular men."

"I guess I fit the bill." There's something familiar about this conversation.

"Yes you do."

Carlita and I talk some more that night and eventually leave together. We go back to my place and after the usual preliminaries and small talk we have sex. She's pretty good in bed. I wasn't at my best for some reason. There was just something wrong with the whole thing. I take her home the next morning. On the way back from her place I was listening to something on the radio and all of sudden I started thinking about Jo. Carlita reminded me of Jo. No wonder I felt strange. I was feeling some guilt about how I treated Jo. I can't treat anybody like that again. It was wrong. It was evil. Carlita's nice, but I don't know about a future between us. It would be wrong to keep anything going with her. I have to stop these one-night stands. They haven't done me any good. I need to find something   real.

Five

"Yo Steve. This babe wants to holler at you," Dave says as we're standing outside during a work break on Thursday morning.

"Yeah? Who is it?"

"Karen."

"Karen? Karen? Oh yeah she's the receptionist in the main office right?"

"Yup that's her. Are you going to holler at her?

"Well...I'm not sure."

Dave winks. "She'll probably give you some."

"Yeah but still. Karen's too damn plain. She's overweight, plain face. Karen's good for somebody, just not me. Maybe that weird brother Rodney can have her."

"Come on man. You can probably get with her tonight if you make an effort."

"I probably could, do I want to though?" I think about Carlita.

"Why wouldn't you? She may not be the most attractive woman but it all looks the same in the dark"

"You got a steady girlfriend Dave?"

"Steady? I got three or four steady girlfriends. There are a lot of lonely women out here. It's up to the fellas to tighten 'em up."

"Three or four huh? Don't you ever just want one?"

"For what? A man's always going to want to have more than one woman. It's our nature."

"We can control our nature. We just have to make to choice to do so."

"Yo what's up with you Steve? You fall in love or something?"

"Naw man. Just thinking."

"Thinking about what? Women are here to be dogged. What else are they good for?"

"You were in love before weren't you?" I ask as an insight came into my mind.

"Me? Hell no! Not the kid. Nawww, I ain't even going to lie like that. I was in love. Serious love too. Back when I was in college. Don't tell nobody... I was a virgin until I was twenty. Then I met this girl named Alicia. She had it all, brains, looks, body. Her butt was phatter than all outdoors. You know what I mean?"

Jessica pops into my mind. "Yeah I know exactly what you mean."

"Man we were into each other for about three months. I ain't never been so happy."

"Then what happened?"

"I found out she was letting my so-called boys hit it. I think I cried like a bitch for three weeks. That was my junior year. I almost dropped out of school because of that shit. After I stopped crying I said I was going to treat women like they want to be treated. They don't want nice guys. All they do is dog nice guys. I ain't cared about no bitch since then. I tell them what they want to hear long enough to get in their panties. Then I kick them to the curb. Fuck them! They act like hoes, I treat them like hoes. Fuck 'em. Bitch ass hoes."

I try to break the mood. "Hey Dave. Break's over. We gotta go back in."

"Yeah man, let's go." Dave has a look on his face that exudes both anger and sadness. Man I can't ever have a look like that. That's too much pain.

****

"Steve, thanks for coming over," Carlita says as I walk through the door of her Tacoma Park apartment. "Have a seat on the couch. Do you want anything to eat or drink? I can fix something real quick."

"No thank you." I unzip my coat and sit down on her couch.

Carlita sits down next to me. "I'm so glad to see you,"

She looks good, very tempting. She'll probably have sex with me right here on the couch.

"Look, I'll get right to the point. This may sound harsh but I don't want to see you."

"What do you mean!?! Did I do something wrong!?!"

"No you didn't do anything wrong. It's me."

"Everybody always says, 'it's me.' when they break up with somebody."

"We were never together Carlita. You're a very attractive young lady, but not for me. I don't see a future for us. All I see is sex and I need more than that."

"I can give you more if you let me," Carlita pleads.

"The vibe isn't there. Straight up, I've been with too many women in too many shallow relationships. I need something based on something stronger than sex. I need a solid foundation. Maybe I would feel differently if we had met under different circumstances. Maybe, maybe not. Whatever the case we can't change the past. What's happened has happened. We do have a choice for the future. I've made my choice."

Carlita looks disgusted. "You know you really sound sincere. Coming in here trying to act like you're so noble. You had a one-night stand and now you want to run away. You want to drop me before I can drop you. Get out of my house. You're nothing but a dog."

"That's what I'm trying to say. I don't want to be a dog. I want to be a man."

"Yeah, yeah. Get out and don't ever call me," Carlita says, trying to gain some control.

"I'm sorry for what happened." I turn and walk out the door.

Carlita slams the door behind me. I hope she has someone to help her through this. I didn't mean to hurt her.

****

I come to the gym to work out and here I am sitting on a locker room bench staring into space. That was tough what I had to do at Carlita's earlier but it had to be done. I can't allow yourself to become like Dave. So much pain and anger. I can't let that destroy me. I...

"What's up bro?" Darryl asks as he stands next to me.

"I didn't hear you come in."

"You didn't work out did you?"

"Naw man."

"Woman?"

"Yeah."

"She dropped you?"

"No I dropped her."

"I guess you did what you had to do."

"Yeah man I did. I would've dogged her. I didn't want to hurt her."

"You're growing I see."

"I want to be like Darryl."

"You don't know how I got to be me."

"You keep saying you had interesting life."

"That I did. I think it's time to tell you about it."

****

Darryl and I are sitting on the bench outside the health club. The night air is cool. It's a star-filled night. Not a cloud in the sky. Darryl stares solemnly at the stars. His face is sad. He speaks.

"I like to stare into the stars, especially when I'm chilling with my lady Sharon. I guess your scruffy butt will have to do.

"My life story. I was born thirty-five years ago to a thirteen-year old mother. My father was some young knucklehead. My mother said I was an accident. I remember that used to make me sad. I used to hate her. Now I understand her better my friend."

"Where is she now?"

"Dead. Drug overdose. My mother wasn't ready for the experience of motherhood. She was living in a foster home when I was born. She had been in several homes by the time I was born. She had never truly been loved I found out later from her last foster parents. She felt a lot of self-hatred. I think she took a lot of it out on me."

"She abused you?" I ask, already suspecting the answer.

Darryl hangs his head. "Yes."

"Well you seem to have turned out all right."

"Not...at first. I lived in foster homes all of my early life. With my mother until she turned eighteen. Then she just left. I was bounced from foster parent to foster parent. Things were all right between the time my mother left and my tenth birthday. My foster parents had four other foster kids. They were good-hearted but they were older and they couldn't keep up with all of us. I started to...hang out with the ...wrong crowd. I hung out with this crew. They were into all sorts of mischief. They had me stealing for them, running love boat. As I got older I started selling drugs."

"Did you sell crack?"

"Naw man this was before crack. Trust me, love boat was just as bad. Love boat had people running down the street buck naked. Yeah I started selling. Making a lot of money. Living large. My foster parents didn't say anything. I guess all the new things I was buying for around the house made them turn a blind eye. Who knows? Maybe they were too scared. They may have been relieved when I moved out. I got buck after that. Running the streets. Getting high. Screwing every girl I could find."

"I guess you got in trouble with the law."

"I had a juvenile record, I always managed to avoid jail though. One time I wasn't so lucky."

"What happened?"

"I was selling drugs in front of this woman's house, Mrs. Barnhill. Church going lady. She lived by herself even though she had grandkids and other relatives come over. Me and my boys used to sit and chill on the wall in her front yard. One day we were sitting out there chilling and she came out and asked us to leave. My boys got up and started to leave. I stood my ground. I told her to go back in the house. She told me she wasn't leaving until I left. Then she got in my face. Then I did something I'll never forgive myself for." A tear formed in Darryl's left eye.

"What?" I'm afraid of the answer.

"I slapped her. Then I hit her. Then when she was down I kicked her. And I kept kicking her. My boys pulled me off. Later one told me I had said, 'I hate you mommy!'"

Man.

Darryl continues. "The police came and took me away. I was charged with assault. Sentenced to serve time in Lorton. Never served for selling drugs but they couldn't let me walk on this one. I was ready for prison. I was tough. Nobody was going to punk me. I had heard prison was like summer camp anyway. I didn't realize that prison would change my life.

"They put me in a cell with this older brother named John. A strong brother, it was his first time being in trouble in his life. He had did everything right. Went to college, spiritual, hard working. He was in for life. He came home early one day to surprise his wife and take her out to dinner. He had made reservations at a fancy restaurant. He adored his wife so much. He worshiped her. That day though he caught her with another man in his bed. John took a gun out of a drawer and shot both of them. John always told me that neither of them deserved to die. It was God's place to judge them, not him.

"John served his time without complaint. He said he deserved his punishment and that God had him there for a reason. We were an odd couple, John was a spiritual man who talked about how God was bigger than our man-made divisions. I was a wild kid full of self-hatred who thought John was crazy. I didn't say anything to him at first. He would talk to me anyway. He would talk about God, politics, race relations, sports, anything.

Eventually, I would talk with him. I told him how I felt about things. Things that I would never share with anybody else."

"He must've had a great effect on you."

"He did. He made me see that I wasn't ordinary. That God lived in my heart. He helped me face my self-hatred. He helped me get my college degree. He introduced me to really getting educated. We would spend hours in the library. You can read a lot in prison. I would read, talk with John, talk with some of the Christian, Muslim, and Kemetic brothers in prison. For the first time in my life my mind was growing. I was growing."

"Is that how you got so wise?"

"Wisdom is gained every day. We learn from everything around us. We just have to be receptive."

"I'm starting to see your point."

"Good. I got out after a while. I remember the day I left. John told me that helping to show me the way was part of his redemption for his crime. John told me, *"Saving your soul is part of my redemption. You, my little brother, you must redeem for your sins. You harmed an old woman, a Black woman, you must pay for that. She was a mother. Her strength has nurtured others. You must redeem yourself for what you have done to her. You have sold drugs that have destroyed your own people. You have destroyed families. You must seek redemption for that for that. As I have help you, you must help another. All the great spiritual teachers taught us to help others so must you. Promise me that you will do that. Promise me, my brother."* I told him yes. John then said, *"As a **Man**, it is your responsibility to keep your word."* Then we hugged. I said, *"Thank you father."* Then I left prison."

I choked back a tear. "Wow."

"I left prison and stayed with a friend that first night. The next day I went to see Mrs. Barnhill. She wouldn't open her door. She told me to leave. I told her I understood, then I told her I was sorry for what I did. Then I broke down and cried on her porch. I kept saying, *"Forgive me, forgive me, please."* It was like years of emotion came out then. Mrs. Barnhill came out and put her arms around me and took me into her house. We've been close ever since. I'm always fixing stuff around her house. She showed me love, and forgiveness. She became the mother I didn't really have. I eventually got a job at a boy's home as a counselor. I try to give them what John and Mrs. Barnhill or as I call her Mama Louise and now Sharon gives me, love. It is my responsibility. That's about it my brother. Learn from my story. Help others. Save someone's life. It is your responsibility, as a **Man**. Later Bro."

Just like that Darryl leaves.

****

"Hello Pops," I say into the phone while sitting on my couch back at my place.

"Steven?" My father asks on the other end. "To what do we owe this pleasure?"

"Pops, can you put mom on the phone?"

"Sure...Mary! Pick up the phone. It Steven!"

My mother picks up the phone. "Steven!?! How are you?"

"I'm fine," I say to both of them. "Look, um, I want to say thank you for taking care of me and raising me right. I love both of you. Thank you for loving me."

255

"We love you too, sweetheart," my mother says.

"Mom, you know I hate when you call me that."

"Okay sweetheart."

"I love you too son," my father says. "I know that I may seem hard sometimes, I did it the only way I knew."

"I know Pops. Thank you."

I spend the next hour telling my parents about what I've been doing lately. It's great to have a family.

Six

Yeah boy! I look good for work today. Bald head looks good. Big and round like Ted says but who cares. It's my head. I'm looking good in my polo shirt and jeans. Today's Friday too. I'm ready to chill out at work. I think I'll leave a little bit early today. Let me make sure everything is turned off. Stove, lights, toilet isn't running. Time to roll. Lock door behind me...hey my neighbor is coming out. Man she's fine. Time to get neighborly. "Hey I guess you're my new neighbor."

"Good morning," she says coldly. She's looking good with a navy-blue dress suit on and some sheer stockings and pumps.

"My name is Steve."

"Laura, pleasure to meet you." She is cold and distant.

We walk to the elevator. "So how do you like the building?"

"It's nice."

The elevator arrives and we both get on. She still has a distant look to her. She almost looks...troubled. I hope I'm not making her feel uncomfortable. I try to lighten the mood. "Ready for the weekend?"

"I guess. I'm supposed to do something with my boyfriend Saturday. No firm plans yet."

Dag she has a boyfriend. It was smooth how she worked it in though. "I'm not sure what I'm doing myself. I might stay in and do some reading."

"That sounds nice," Laura says as the elevator stops on the lobby level.

"Well see you later neighbor." I get off the elevator. She isn't moving. She must have a car in the garage.

I go on to work. I have a feeling that it's going to be an interesting day.

****

"So what's going on for the weekend?" I ask Gloria and Dave as I go through my documents.

Gloria looks up from her computer. "I'm spending time with my husband and going to church on Sunday. You're invited to come."

"Not this weekend. Soon maybe." I don't know if I'm ready yet. I still have some stuff to work out. "What about you Dave?"

"I'm going out on dates Saturday and Sunday," Dave says.

"You need to be going to church, young man," Gloria says with a look of mock sternness.

"I'm not a church goer, Ms. Gloria."

"You can still try it out and stop with this 'Ms. Gloria' stuff. Makes me sound old."

"Yes ma'am," Dave says in all seriousness. Dave's a trip. He acts like women are so bad and yet he's very respectful of older women. "What are you doing this weekend Steve?"

"I'm going to do some reading. Black history and stuff."

"No dates?"

"I'm trying to chill out some. Get my head together."

"Aw man, please," Dave smirks.

"Good for you Steve," Gloria smiles. "Get yourself together first and the right woman will come along."

"Oh please," Dave says.

"Oh hush," Gloria says.

We spend the rest of the day working. Around four in the afternoon, Fred calls me into his office and closes the door. I wonder what this is about. I had spoken casually with Fred before today. Talked about different things. I wonder what he wants now. I hope this isn't a layoff. We still have plenty of work. I know my work has improved over the past few weeks.

"Calm down Steve," Fred says as he sits down. "You look like you're about to lose your job."

"Naw I'm alright." Whoo! What a relief.

"I see that your work is improving."

"Thank you. Gloria helped me out there."

"She's like that. Her husband is lucky to have her."

"So is everything else alright?"

"Yes and no. Yes as far as this company and the work you're doing for it is concerned. Not as far as your future."

"What do you mean?" I'm confused by Fred's statement.

"I mean you're doing some good work for the company, however, you do want to go beyond coding?"

"Well yes. I'd rather be doing paralegal work. Things that are more challenging."

"We have some paralegal positions that will be opening up in the future. In-house employees get first preference."

"Great, I'll apply when a position comes up."

"You're qualified to get a position from what I've seen on your resume."

"Yesss!"

"Hold on now. Decisions aren't made just from resumes. Supervisors check people out from a distance. How you look to them is more important than what is on a piece of paper. That's what I wanted to talk to you about, your image."

"My image?"

"Yes your image. You have on a polo shirt and jeans. That's all right because everybody else is casual. However, if you want to move up in this company you have to dress the part."

"I get what you're saying."

"Good. Remember perception is important. If you look like a file clerk, people will treat you like a file clerk. If you look like an executive, people treat you like an executive. So Monday morning I want you to come in here with a professional shirt, neck tie, creased slacks and shined shoes. Consider it a career move."

"I'll do that."

"Good now get back to work before this break brings down your production."

I stand up to shake Fred's hand. "Thanks man."

"My pleasure." Fred shakes my hand. "Do the same for somebody else."

****

Ah what a workout! I should work out on Saturday mornings more often. Then again it's easy to do since I didn't party last night. I remember the day when I couldn't stay in on a Friday night to save my life. Now look at me. I guess I'm getting old. Ah this stretching feels good. Yes, that hits the spot. Gym's pretty empty on a Saturday morning. Just me...wow who's that! Haven't seen her around here before but then I don't come in the morning. Nice young lady. Nice light-brown complexion, bright light-brown-eyes, slim face, nice button nose, nice lips, nice breasts, stomach, butt, legs. Man I should...leave her alone. Probably have sex with her for a few weeks and then get dumped. I'll leave her al...

"Good morning," Bright Eyes says to me.

"Morning," I try to act like everything is cool.

Bright Eyes sits down and stretches. "This is the first time I've seen you here."

"I've been a member of the gym for a while." I'm still amazed that a woman this fine approached me first.

Bright eyes extends her hand. "My name is Monica Townes."

"Steve Walters." She has soft hands.

"So what do you do Steve?"

"I work for a litigation support company, WPR."

"You have an interesting job?"

"It's alright."

Monica shows genuine interest. "Litigation support sounds like it's fun. Are you in the courtroom all the time?"

"Naw, all I do is code documents. I do all the tedious stuff that has to be done before going to court."

"It still sounds interesting. Any job can be exciting if you use your imagination." Monica spreads her legs and stretches to her right knee. All the time never taking her eyes off of me.

"So what do you do?"

"I'm an actress," Monica says proudly as she stretches towards her left knee.

"An actress? Wow. Have you ever been on T.V.?"

"In a few commercials. I'm rehearsing for a play now though. It will open at the Lincoln Theater late next month. It's called, *Virtuoso*."

"Virtuoso?"

"Yes, it's about this woman being pursued by these two spiritually powerful men. One good, one evil. I play the lead character, a woman named Cyndra Mckie who has great spiritual strength herself. Only problem is that Cyndra doesn't realize her gifts."

"So is this something about psychic ability?"

"Not quite. It's not that metaphysical. It's really deep. You have to come see it."

"Since you're in it I will."

"I can get you and your girlfriend good seats."

"I'm not seeing anyone."

Monica's eyes get brighter. "Would you be interested in seeing a play with me next week, *The Spot*?"

"I'd love to." Dag she's picking me up. I'm gonna tear her up. Wait I can't do that. We'll go as friends. I won't try anything.

"Glad to hear it. We can exchange phone numbers before you leave. Set everything up for next week."

"That'll be fine with me." This beautiful woman asked me out. I gotta call my mother.

Seven

"Man that was a game!" Ted yells after we finish watching the Wizards beat the Knicks on T.V. on this Sunday afternoon.

"The Wizards winning. Ain't that some stuff," Ray says while sitting in an easy chair chilling.

"Hey that's alright," I say. "Y'all gotta play the Sixers next. So y'all better celebrate now."

"Forget you," Ted says while getting up to get a soda.

"So what's up today Steve?" Ray says while half-watching the television.

"Not much. After I leave here I'm going home and catching up on some reading."

"Yeah? So what'cha reading?"

"I'm reading this book on African-American history."

"Uh oh. Phil got to you."

"Naw man I had an interest anyway."

"Forget history. I'm more interested in the future," Ted says as he walks in with a grape soda.

"History's important," I point out. "We study the past so we don't make the same mistakes in the future."

Ted sits on the couch. "I look forward to better things in the future."

"Just like a salesman," Ray says. "Always optimistic."

"Gotta keep hope up. What about you Steve? What do you think about the future?" Ted asks.

"I don't know to tell you the truth. You remember how I was. For the longest time I was drifting. Going nowhere. I'm moving forward now but I still don't know where I'm going."

"At least you're going in the right direction," Ray says. "So many brothers are stuck in neutral. They either don't know where to go or how to get there, or what to do if they get there. At least you have an idea. You have a college degree, Ted has a masters, I'm about to get my MBA."

"Oh man Ray, You're going to start that education thing again," I joke.

"Man, shut up. You know education is important. You wouldn't have went to college."

"You're right."

"Education is the key. That's why I'm always on you. That's what my family instilled in me. They told me that with education I can control my life," Ray says.

"Education is the key," Ted says with a serious tone. "There are so many knuckleheads out there who don't see the value of an education. They think that they can get by with just "street smarts." They think that they can get over. Those fools are stupid and they're too ignorant to realize it."

"Preach brother," I say.

"Say it reverend," Ray adds.

"I know I joke around a lot but I'm serious when it comes to the future. I bust my ass every day to make sure my future is the way I want it," Ted says.

I nod my head. "You are a working hard man."

"Have to," Ted says. "So what are you going to do Steve? Are you going to go to law school or something?"

"I'm thinking about it man." I'm sincere. "I'm thinking about it seriously."

****

Saturday night. I'm on my way to pick up Monica. She lives over on Massachusetts Ave. near American University. She is so nice. I haven't met a woman this easy to talk to since Jessica, not even Randi. She's probably the first woman I can just sit and listen to. For Monica everything is an adventure. Even going to the bus stop in the morning. She can be so dramatic about everything. It feels good to have her as a friend.

We're going to see a play at the Lincoln Theater, *The Spot.* I heard it was good. The critics loved it, which is saying something. Man I can't believe that I'm actually going on a platonic date. Everything is cool with Monica. I told her everything about my past relationships. My wicked past as I call it. What got me was that Monica was so understanding. She said that people shouldn't

266

judge each other. She said that we all have done things that we're less than proud of. She said that we have to learn from these bad experiences in order to turn them into something good. Yes I think we'll make great friends.

This feels like it's going to be a good night. I have on my light-gray double breasted Italian cut suit. Had to have it taken in though. The last time I wore it I was at 240. I'm fifty pounds lighter and I'm feeling better as a result.

I'm almost there. Let me pull into her building's driveway. Who's that! That girl is fine! That girl is...Monica!?! Damn she's fine. I haven't seen her since Wednesday evening at the Gym. That form fitting navy dress coming down to her ankles and those pumps make her look good. Oh man she looks like totally different with her hair out and some makeup on. I'm going to have to rethink this platonic thing.

I get out and walk to the other side of the car to hold the door for Monica. She thanks me as she gets in and I close the door.

"So how was your day today?" I ask as we leave her building's driveway.

"Same as always."

"Uh oh. What happened?" For most people "same as always" means their day was uneventful. For Monica it's an action-adventure movie.

"Oh the usual," Monica says wistfully. "I'm walking to the theater for rehearsal looking grungy. I'm thinking 'nobody will bother me' when this gold-tooth man...boy...something, with two matching earrings...they looked better than mine...said, 'Good Morning.' I speak when people speak to me on the street so I just said 'hi' without really thinking about it and kept going. Then the man...boy...whatever said, 'Come here girl. You look good. Can I lay on top of you?' I'm thinking that instead of spending money on that matching gold tooth and earrings he should've invested in glasses because I was looking ugly. Bums were looking at me as if to say, "Damn she looks awful." Anyway I said, 'No thank you,' even though I really wanted to say a lot more. Then, even though the man...boy...bama could see that I wasn't interested in talking to him, he had to say the one word near and dear to women everywhere."

I play the straight man. "Which word is that?"

"He called me a bitch. Nice and calmly I walked back...got in his face...stepped back...he had some bad breath. He could afford a gold tooth, better earrings than I had and he couldn't pay 50 cents for some breath mints.

"I like how you go off on these tangents."

"Shut up and drive. After I moved back two yards. His breath...I wish I had a bullhorn...I reminded him that I'm the same as his mother, his sister, his cousin...I would have said his daughter, but he was ugly with bad breath so I didn't think he had one."

"Dag."

"Bad breath was speechless. I turned and left. Men. If we could keep you locked in a closet until we needed you."

"You know you love us."

"All because of a cruel joke."

"You know I should introduce you to my boy Ted. Y'all probably get along like brother and sister."

****

We get to the Lincoln Theater to see the play. Called *The Spot*, it's about this apartment where all sorts of weird people run in and out. This one character cracked me up. Cuz just sat in a chair the whole play watching TV. He didn't move, didn't speak, just sat there. All hell was breaking loose on the stage and Cuz was oblivious to it all. The whole thing was funny. Afterwards Monica and I go to get some food at this restaurant on U Street. Food was good, conversation was better. Finally we make it back to Monica's building.

"That was a great time. Thanks for coming to see the play with me," Monica says.

"My pleasure."

Monica has a seductive look in her eyes. "Do you have to go so soon? You can come up and chat for a little while. Listen to some music."

"Naw I better go." Girl don't do this to me.

"I won't bite… unless you want me to," Monica says slow and seductively.

"I thought we said we were going to be platonic?" Those words came out of my mouth?

Monica breaks into a smile. "I know. Giving you something to think about."

"Get out of my car. Seriously though I had a good time and I look forward to many more in the future."

"Me too," Monica says as she gets out of my car. "I think the future will be full of surprises. Bye Steve. Give me a call tomorrow."

"Bye Monica. Talk to you tomorrow."

Eight

Another Friday. Another day sitting in Fred's Office.

"You're probably wondering why you're here," Fred says after he closes the door and takes a seat behind his desk.

"Well it did cross my mind." Now what?

Fred isn't showing any emotion. "By the way, you look nice in your shirt and tie."

"Thanks. I took your advice."

"Good that somebody listens to me."

"Well you're an old guy, I figure you know these things." He's not smiling.

"Steve I knew this day was coming."

"What's up?" I don't like the tone of this.

"Steve you're leaving here..."

"Ah man. I thought I was doing alright."

"Don't interrupt me. You're leaving here and going to work on a project at the Department of Justice."

"The Justice Department? We have a contract with them?"

"We have a contract with damn near everybody."

"Man I'm being transferred. What will I be doing?"

"As far as I know it's something related to narcotics. I don't know anything other than that. I do know that you'll be doing more substantive paralegal work."

I fake like I'm sad. "I'm going to miss coding."

"Yeah right. Anyway kid, you start down at the Main Justice building on Monday. I'll find out where exactly you'll be reporting this afternoon."

"Thanks man," I say as I stand up.

Fred walks around the table to shake my hand. "No problem, I try to be of service."

"Yo man thanks for everything."

"My pleasure. Don't embarrass me down there."

"You got it man."

"Oh and come back to visit."

"I don't know...it's kinda far."

Fred finally cracks a smile. "It's down the street. Get out of here."

****

"Hey Gloria, Dave, I'm going to the Justice Department on Monday. I'm going to be doing paralegal work. No more coding." I take a seat at my computer

"That's a relief," Gloria smiles. "I don't have to clean up any more of your mess."

"Now Gloria you know my work has got better."

"Just teasing. Congratulations."

"Thanks Gloria."

"Yeah congratulations Steve," Dave says. "I didn't think you had it in you."

"Thanks for the vote of confidence."

"I would be jealous if I wanted to move up in this company."

"Speaking of which, what business are you working on today?" Dave hadn't mentioned any business schemes lately.

"I'm thinking about starting a dating service for all the singles out there."

"All they need to do is go to church," Gloria adds without looking up from her computer.

"There are a lot of singles out there who don't go to church, Ms. Gloria," Dave answers.

"Maybe they wouldn't be single if they went to church," Gloria tells Dave.

"You'll see ma'am," Dave says.

"I'm going to miss you two," I say.

Lunch time. Waited until now to speak with Gloria alone. There she is. "Hey Gloria wait up."

"Hi Steve. Where are you headed for lunch?"

"I'm going over to *The Shops*. Let me treat you to lunch."

"Thank you. So what did I do to deserve this?" Gloria blushes.

"A couple of months ago you went out of your way to help me with my work. This is the least I can do."

"No you can do what I told you last time. Help somebody out in the future."

"So I don't need to buy you lunch?"

"Now I didn't say that. I'm ready to eat. Let's go." Gloria grabs my arm and leads me out of the building.

****

Oh what a day. I get a promotion and I get to visit Monica tonight. If only this elevator would move faster. Finally! I'm on my floor. I gotta get in and change. I...what do we have here? "Hi Laura."

"Hi Steve," Laura says.

"Heading out tonight?"

"I don't know...depends on my boyfriend."

"Y'all have any big plans?"

"No he'll probably come over about ten o'clock and chill out like he always does."

"He's probably tired from working all day."

"Him? Jordan? He doesn't have a job. Not for the last couple of weeks anyway."

"So what does he do during the day?"

"Nothing really. He sits around his mom's house watching TV. How can a 32 year old man not have a job and still live with his mom?"

"Well...could be a lot of things."

"Tell me."

"Hey look, you want to come inside for a few minutes. You look like you need to talk," I say as I motion towards my apartment.

"Sure why not."

We go in the apartment and Laura has a seat on the couch. Before I can ask her if she wants something to eat or drink she starts talking.

"I don't know what it is I see in Jordan. He has no ambition. Has never been to college. Has never lasted a year on a job. Lives with his mother and doesn't do anything around there besides eat and sleep."

There's something familiar about this. "Do you love him?"

"The sad part is that I am in love with him,"

"Let me guess, Jordan, that's his name right?"

"Yes."

"Jordan's this big fine brother. The kind that has women swooning all over him."

"Actually Jordan is not very attractive."

"So how did you fall in love with him?"

"He was different. He acted like he really cared. He didn't act like he was intimidated by me."

"Why would anybody be intimidated by you? You're very beautiful and you seem like you're smart."

"Thanks for the compliment. My so-called good looks were the problem. All my life I've had people telling me how beautiful I was. Ever since I hit puberty I had people hit on me. Men and women. Even some of my cousins would try to have sex with me. A couple even…" Laura gets real quiet. Aw shit.

"Were you molested?"

Laura didn't answer. The look on her face speaks volumes. We sit quietly for a few minutes before she speaks. "I started to become withdrawn. I stayed to myself and studied all the time."

"What about your friends? Did you hang out? Engage in any activities?"

"I danced with this troupe. Even then I stayed to myself. So many girls used to hate me. I don't know why."

I remember Jessica telling me the same thing. "A friend told me a long time ago that women get jealous of other women because of their looks."

"People have always told me that I'm beautiful…I never believed them."

"Why not?"

Laura looks like she's about to cry. "Because everybody was so mean to me."

Laura is silent for a few moments as she takes time to regain her composure. She continues. "I had never had a boyfriend. Went all the way through high school and college without one. Then I met Jordan last year. He approached me on the street. He was different from the other people that tried to approach me on the street. He wasn't rude. He walked up to me and introduced himself. We started going out after that. I fell in love with him later on."

"So what happened to make you sad?"

"After I told him that I was in love with him he changed. It's like he knew he had me."

"What did he do?"

"He became abusive. He would tell me that I wasn't shit. That I thought I was all that. That I wasn't smart. All sorts of things."

"Why do you stay with him?"

"He was the only one who wanted me."

"Don't believe that."

"You don't know how it was like."

"Maybe I don't but there's always hope."

"Perhaps...I better get out of here. Jordan will be over in a little while."

"Okay," I get up from the couch and lead Laura to the door. "If you ever need to talk again just knock on the door."

"Thanks Steve. I really appreciate this."

"No problem." I open the door to let Laura out. Laura has a smile on her face for the first time.

Nine

What a morning. First day on the new project. They're not playing. No ceremony. No showing me around the office. I'm right in the middle of things. Good thing I'm a sharp brother or I couldn't handle it. I wonder where I'll eat today. They have a lot food places around here. Man there's some nice looking women around here. Now she has some nice legs.

"Still checking out the ladies?" a voice asks behind me.

Who? "Yo Joe what's up man."

"Just chilling as you used to say," Joe says as he walks up and hugs me. "Almost didn't recognize you. You must have been on that serious diet or you have some virus."

"Naw man, working out in the gym."

"You're looking good Steve. Got a shirt and tie on too. Where are you working now?"

"I'm working for WPR Company. They have a contract with the Department of Justice. I'm working with the Criminal Division. If I tell you anymore I'll have to kill you."

"All right, all right, I understand."

"Yeah man I started this morning. I was transferred from a coding project with WPR. So what are you doing for yourself?"

"I'm doing some court-appointed work at the courthouse as well as some other things."

"You said you were going to get your own thing going."

"I'm a man of my word."

"That's true. Speaking of which, are you having anymore parties?"

"Still a party man?"

"I don't get out as much as I used to but I try to go to quality parties."

"And those are what I give. I'll have another one soon. You still at the same number."

"Naw man I moved to 16th Street last year. I'll give you my new number."

"Tell you what. Here's my card." Joe reaches into his wallet to get a business card. "Give me a call."

I take the card from Joe. "Bet."

"So do you like your job?"

"It nice."

"You want something else?"

"You got a job?"

"As a matter of fact I do. I'm expanding my business and I'm going to need a legal assistant. Somebody who knows what they're doing and somebody I can trust. Are you interested?"

"Depends on how much you're paying."

"I'll start you at a good salary. More as we get more business."

"I don't know. I really wanted to work with a firm," I joke.

"Forget that," Joe says in all seriousness. "You can be on the ground floor of a new firm. One you can become a partner in once you get out of law school."

"I haven't decided to go to law school."

"Are you thinking about it?"

"Actually I have been thinking about my future lately."

"That's a step in the right direction. What about my job offer?"

"I'll take it. I have to give WPR two weeks' notice."

"That's great. Good to have you aboard."

"Glad to be there."

Joe changes the subject. "So how are the ladies treating you?"

"Just chilling. Trying to get my head together. Took a while to get to this position. Women can mess up the process sometimes. What about you man? Still a player?"

"Had to slow down. My womanizing ways weren't compatible with my religious beliefs. I've been dealing with one lady the last couple of months. Her name is Lisa. She goes to my church. Do you belong to a church?"

"Not yet man, not yet."

"You're invited out to mine whenever you're ready. In the meantime just take care of your business so you can work with me free and clear."

"Alright man."

"I gotta get back to court now and convince a jury that this young boy didn't know that he had a kilo of cocaine in his backpack."

"Holler at you later Joe." A new job. Life is getter better.

****

"Congratulations Steve," Monica says after I tell her about my encounter with Joe today and his job offer. She's sitting here in my apartment with a T-shirt and sweats on. She looks "grimy" as she calls it. Even grimy she is more beautiful than a lot of women I've seen.

"Thanks, It's amazing how things seem to be going right for me," I respond. We're just sitting here chilling, half watching some dumb show on television.

"You're creating your own opportunities. If you're going in the right direction, things will happen to keep you in the right direction."

"That's funny. Darryl from the gym said the same thing."

"It's been said a thousand different ways but it's the same principle. You have to believe in a goal, then focus on getting there. Then when opportunities come you have to seize them. Remember though, you always have to keep your eyes open."

"So have you been practicing what you preach?" I put Monica on the spot.

"Of course I have. It started when I was in high school..."

"Is this going to be one of your stories?"

"Shut up and listen. You might learn something. The acting bug bit me my junior year in high school. So I went out for this Christmas show. The Christmas show consisted of comedy skits, songs from the glee club, and numbers from the school band. So I auditioned and got a role with only two words."

"I bet you were mad."

"Not at all. I didn't have any experience acting and was grateful to be there. In a way though you are right. I didn't want my parents to come to the play just to hear their daughter say two words. I decided to take steps to increase my roles in the show."

"So what did you do? Knock off other people and take their parts?"

"Not quite...almost."

"This I gotta hear."

"Then stop interrupting me." Monica sweetly bats her eyelashes. "I watched every skit being rehearsed and learned everybody's lines, even the guys. I prepared myself to take anybody's place at a moment's notice. Then my opportunity came. First a guy who had a big part in one of the skits missed rehearsal. The director didn't play that. So he was like, 'Does anybody know Gene's lines?' I was like, 'I do. I know them by heart.' The director then said, 'Good, get up here then and don't mess up.' I got up there and played the part better than Gene."

"So you played a man?"

"No silly, the part could have been played by anybody. Anyway I had that two word part, I had Gene's part which consisted of delivering onion rings."

"Onion rings?"

"Onion rings. We were doing a parody of the 12 days of Christmas. Instead of five golden rings. I had five golden onion rings."

I chuckle.

Monica continues. "Anyway I was content at that point. Then the director surprised me by giving me the narrator part in this parody we did on the president at that time."

"That must have been funny."

"If nothing else the Republican presidents were good for laughs. Anyway since then I've always placed myself in a position to get good roles. Also to get good temp jobs when I wasn't acting."

"Sounds like you have everything all worked out."

"I try. If you really want to be my friend though, you'll workout my neck."

"Let me guess you want me to massage your neck?"

Monica sits on the floor between my legs. "Thanks, I thought you would never offer me one."

"My pleasure." I begin massaging her neck.

"Harder." Monica was obviously getting into it.

"Yes mistress."

I massage Monica's neck and shoulders for about twenty minutes. Then she quietly sits up on the couch and we silently look at each other and lightly brush our lips together. I stop before we go any further.

"Steve, what's wrong? Is it my breath?"

"No it's not that."

"Good because I brush after meal and use plenty of mouthwash."

"Monica it's…I really care for you as a friend. I really don't want to mess that up. For too long all my relationships with women have been sexual. I'm tired of that. I know that sounds weird coming from man."

"No…everybody needs more than sex. It's good that you recognize that. We can be more if you want or we can just be friends. I enjoy being around you."

"Do you?"

"Yes I do. Why don't we relax for now? Just hold me."

"Okay." I stretch out on the couch and Monica stretches out with me.

Nice and comfortable. I can get used to this.

Ten

What a morning. One more day and a half until the weekend. Six and a half more days until I leave WPR Company. I'm really going to miss Gloria and Dave. Last time I talked to him he was talking about starting a publishing company. What kinda brother would try to start a publishing company? Dave always has some scheme going. Cuz is a trip. I hope he makes it. I hope everybody makes it.

I wonder what I'll get to eat at *The Shops*. I think I'll get some chicken and fries from *Papa's Chicken*. Hmmm, that brother looks familiar. Oh man! I haven't seen Cuz since college. Let me catch up to him. It seems like I'm seeing a lot of people while hanging out in the streets. "Yo Tommy!"

Tommy turns around and sees me and walks towards me grinning. Tommy's a big muscle headed brother. I remember joking with him in college that he was using steroids. He would just attribute his size to his upbringing in rural Louisiana.

"Hey boah! What're ya doing in D.C.? I thought you were in Philly," Tommy says as he walks over and bear hugs me. "Looks like you put on some muscle."

"Actually I've lost some weight. You're the one who had the muscles."

"So what are you in D.C. for? You didn't answer my question boah," Tommy grins. Tommy always had one of those ear to ear grins. Like he had some good gumbo.

"I work here. I've been here for seven years. Been working as a paralegal. What are you doing here with your red beans and rice eating self?"

"Don't mention red beans and rice boah. Haven't had any since I've been in town. I'm here temporally with a media consulting company. Been here for two weeks."

"Cuz we gotta hang out."

"I wish I'd known you was here 'cause I'm leaving to go back to New Aw'lins tonight."

"So that's where you're living now?"

"Yup. For two years."

"How're things in your hometown?"

"Everything's aww right. Go home every weekend for Sunday dinner."

"Still a big mama's boy huh?"

"If you ate my mama's cooking you would be my mama's boy too."

"Maybe, but she can't cook like my mother."

"We should have a contest one day. The best mama's cooking. Whoever can make us loosen our belts the most wins."

"Bet, we definitely have to do that. Say, what are you doing now?

"Nothing. Why?"

"Let's get something to eat in here."

"Sounds good."

We go into *The Shops* and get something to eat from *Papa's*. We find a place to sit down. After a few bites we reminisce about old times.

"You remember when we won the intramural football championship our junior year boah?" Tommy asks.

"Do I? That championship game was crazy. We were down twelve points with five minutes left."

"Then Vince got that interception and ran it back for a touchdown. That was one fast white boy."

"He wasn't white. He was Italian. He made sure everybody made that distinction."

"That was some game. On the next series I made a sack and then the next play you got an interception."

"That was something. That's when Jimmy took over with his trash talking self. He took us from end to end. I remember when Mark caught that winning touchdown with three seconds left."

"He caught it on his knees. That was pretty."

"Then we partied like crazy afterwards."

"Hey whatever happened to trash-talking Jimmy? Cuz was always talking some smack. Always pushing people to go the extra step."

"Ol' blondie is a motivational speaker getting six figures."

"Talk about somebody suited for their profession."

We talked about who did what. Who's married to who? Who got kids? One subject we didn't bring up I decided to broach.

"Yo Tommy, you remember that girl I was real tight with, Jessica? You hear anything about her?"

"You mean you don't know?"

"Know what." I didn't like his tone.

"Jessica committed suicide two years ago."

****

Jessica's dead. I can't believe she's dead. Only woman that I've ever truly loved and she's dead. Why God why? Tommy said he heard the news from Charmaine. Apparently Devon messed her head up and then dumped her. She started using drugs, was homeless, and got into prostitution. Funny, she told me those same things in that dream a while ago. That's scary. She was dead then. That is so doggone spooky. Maybe I really was headed down the same path that she headed. I don't know.

How could she even go down that path? From what she told me she had a loving family, never missed anything growing up. She said her parents never argued. Her and her sisters got along well. I wonder what can make it all go so wrong. From what she told me Jessica's parents did everything they could to insure that she was raised properly. She went to church, got involved in activities. Left the guys alone while she was in high school. I guess going to an all-girl school helped her in that regard. Maybe that's what was wrong. She really wasn't exposed to men until she was in college. Then again is that really an excuse? There is no possible way that we can be exposed to everything as we grow up. Our parents can only do so much. They're only human. Jessica's parents did everything they could and she still ended up at the bottom.

Why? Why did she have to end up where she did? Who does she blame? Does she blame all those dogs she slept with? No, I don't think she can. Not one of them forced her to do anything. Not one. Everything Jessica did was her decision. Her choice. Choose. That's it. That was the meaning of that dream. I thought that the dream meant making a choice between staying in the gutter and making a decision to achieve greatness. The meaning was deeper than that. Everything that happens to us is a matter of choice. We have the power to choose how life affects us. When Jessica rejected me, I chose to let it get me down. I could have chosen to learn from the situation and grow. Instead I chose to let the situation hold me back. Everything is a choice. Even love, despite what people may think. I chose to love Jessica. I could have as easily chose not to love her. Wow this is so deep.

God gave everybody a great gift in giving us the ability to make choices. Unfortunately, many of us don't use that gift. We follow others. Then again we even make a choice to follow others. We can just as easily choose to be leaders. I'm going to choose to be a leader.

I'm going to miss Jessica. I wish I could have done something for her. Maybe I could have but the past can't be changed. I choose to learn from the past and grow. I choose to be a leader. I choose to make a difference. Jessica...I know that you're with...a special man...now. I'll always remember you. In honor of your memory, I choose to do whatever I can to help prevent others from going down the path that you took. The path that I almost took. I choose to help others to make that choice.

Rest in peace Jessica. Thank you for helping me to make my choice.

Eleven

Yes, Yes, Yes, Everything is going so well through my first week working with Joe. Real paralegal work. I actually enjoy looking up cases in a law library. I remember when I couldn't stand doing that. Now I'm looking forward to it. Maybe because of all that tedious coding and what not that I've been doing for all of these litigation support companies. Then again it's probably my attitude. I'm choosing to enjoy all of my experiences. No more complaining and feeling sorry for myself. I'm choosing to truly make something of myself and man does it feel good.

Friday night and sitting in the place chilling. That Pat Methany piece is kicking. *And the truth will always be.* I can listen to that song all day. What can I get into tonight? I should read something, chill out by myself. Now that's something. I still think about the times when I had to go out. I used to hate sitting around this hole in wall. Now I enjoy sitting around this hole in wall. Too bad Monica isn't here tonight but she has to rehearse for that play. I can't wait t...

Knock, Knock, Knock.

Who the hell is that? "Who is it!?!"

"It's me, Laura," says the voice from the other side.

"Hold on I'm coming." Do I look alright? T-shirt, old shorts, smelly socks. Yeah I'm alright.

I open the door. "Hey." Laura didn't look so good. She looks sad and depressed. Hair isn't fixed. No makeup. Sweats. We both look equally messed up. Except I'm smiling. "What's up? You don't look so good. Come in, come in, have a seat."

"Thank you." Laura comes in and sits down on my couch.

I point to the kitchen. "You want anything to eat or drink?"

"No thank you."

I sit down next to Laura on the couch. "So what did he do?"

"How do you know Jordan did something?"

I look at her.

"He dumped me!" Laura says as tears stream down her face.

I instinctively put my arms around her. She buries her head in my chest and cries more.

Laura cries for about ten minutes and then holds her head up and wipes her face with her hands. I get up to find some tissue for her out of my bathroom. I come back and give it to her. I sit down and allow her to regain her composure. Then she speaks.

"Jordan told me last night that he was tired of me. He said that I was smothering him."

"Were you?"

"I...I don't think so. I wanted him to spend more time with me. To call me more. I gave him all the space he wanted. Last night he decided to leave me. Why? He didn't really say. He said I was smothering him."

"I wish I could give you an answer but to be honest with you he didn't seem like all that anyway."

"B...but he made me happy."

"He didn't make you happy all the time though."

"He made me happier than anybody else. He didn't act like he was scared of me."

"That still doesn't mean that he was good for you."

"Whether he was good or bad for me he was still there. No matter how mean he got he could still be nice. It was still nice to be held. Nobody else wanted to hold me. Now I'm alone."

"You're not alone. You have me."

"You're here now, but how long is that going to last. You'll get a girlfriend and won't be here for me. Watch."

"Don't you have other friends?"

"I told you how other people were around me. The men always make crude remarks or come-ons and the women are always jealous."

"That's only because people haven't got know you. You seem to be...distant."

"I grew to be that way."

"You have to open up more."

"I don't...know. I don't even care. Jordan's gone. The only man to have made me happy is gone."

"Get another one."

"It's not that simple. I love him."

"I know how it feels to be in love and lose that love. You have to go on. Take things one day at a time."

"I don't know if I can."

"I'll help you."

"You will?"

"Yes."

"Why?"

"Everybody needs a friend and I'll be yours."

"Thank you. Nobody has told me that before."

"Well I'm telling you now. So sit back and chill. Keep me company tonight. We can check out a stupid T.V. Show."

We spend the rest of the evening watching T.V. and getting to know each other. I can get used to this friendship thing.

Twelve

"Yo Darryl wait up!" I run to catch up with Darryl outside of the gym. I saw him for a few minutes but I didn't get to really talk with him. I've had a lot on my mind lately and I need somebody to talk to.

"Hello sir. You seem like you have something urgent on your mind. Have seat in my office." Darryl sits down on the bench outside of the health club.

I sit down. "Yeah man I do have a lot on my mind."

"Let it go then. Is it work?"

"Work? Naw. For the first time in a long time I enjoy going to work. I feel good working hard."

"Good for you then. The problem must be women."

"As always you hit it right on the head. Three of them are in the picture in different ways."

"Okay tell me about them one at a time."

"First there's this young lady named Jessica. She was my best friend in college but...I lost contact with her after college. I found out last week that she that she died."

"That must have been rough to hear."

"Naw man it gets even rougher. A few months ago right before I started shaving my head she appeared to me in a dream. She basically told me to get my life together."

"A lot of people have dreams like that."

"She died a couple of years ago."

"Oh. You know it's funny. There is so much out there that we have no real understanding of but these things still exist. Before you shaved your head you were headed in the wrong direction. Maybe this...Jessica, came to you in a dream to save you. Maybe because she was the one person that you would listen to. I know some folks who practice African Traditional Religions who talk about Ancestors coming to them in dreams. Even old school Christians from the south talk about seeing their loved ones in dreams."

"It did wake me up. It was so weird though. In the dream she told me how she had got involved in drugs, homelessness and prostitution. When I heard about her death...I found out that she had been involved in drugs, homelessness, and prostitution."

"Fascinating. How did she die?"

"Suicide."

"Sorry to hear that. For someone to get to a point where they would take their own life is tragic."

"Tell me about it. I'll miss her even though I know she's in a better place."

"Amen to that."

"Which brings me to the next lady...my next door neighbor, Laura. I'm worried about her."

"Why's that?"

"Her boyfriend dumped her last week and she's been alternating between being very happy and being very sad."

"Being dumped is hard for most women. Women are not as used to rejection as men are in this society. So when it happens they typically cannot handle it."

"Tell me about it. The thing is I'm worried about her especially after I found out about Jessica."

"You're not developing any romantic feelings for her are you?"

"No I see her as a friend which brings me to the third lady, Monica."

"Oh yes Miss Townes. I've spoken to her several times."

"Monica's my girl. We can talk about anything but...but..."

"You wonder if you should risk the friendship by taking it to another level."

"Exactly."

"Well that depends on what you want from her. If all you want is a fling don't do it because it would jeopardize the friendship."

"I don't want her for a fling. I can see something long term with Monica."

"So go for it. What's the problem?"

"What if it ends like all of my other relationships?"

"It could. You can also end up with happiness for a lifetime."

"I still don't know if I want to risk the friendship with Monica."

"By taking the risk you can have something greater. There was a man who had terrible luck with women. They rejected him for every reason imaginable. They called him every name in the book. Told him he was ugly. Called him broke for not having enough money. Told him he didn't have a future. He would get rejected but you know what? He never gave up, he persevered. He was rejected by 99 women. Number one hundred didn't reject him. She was everything a man could want. Beautiful, intelligent, caring, you name it she had it. The man found his happiness. He forgot about the 99 women who rejected him. The man found the right one. As for the 99 women, they became jealous. The man they had rejected got a well-paying job with a bright future and even improved his looks. He was able to treat the right woman like a queen simply because she believed in him."

"That's a deep story. Is it true?"

"It's true for somebody. One more thing that you should remember about relationships. One great relationship beats out 100 bad relationships. So what are you going to do about Miss Townes?"

"I'm going to go for it. It's about time I got into a happy relationship."

"Good for you Steve. I see that you're spiraling."

"Spiraling?"

"Spiraling. You ever see a spiral staircase?

"Yeah. A family friend has one in the middle of their house in Philly."

"Life is like a spiral staircase inside a building. You're either climbing the steps to the top floor or you are going down to the basement."

I nod my head. "That's where my life was the past couple of years. I went down the stairs to the basement. Now I'm climbing up the stairs back to the top. Thanks for helping me go in the right direction."

"You're welcome but all I did was shine a light. You're the one who climbed in the right direction. Keep climbing."

"That I will do."

****

I'm enjoying this play, *Virtuoso*. It's about these two spiritually powerful men, they both have genius-level intellects, great charisma and they even look powerful. One, Theodore Spencer, is an attorney who helps the poor, he's always helping the little guy. The other man is Alexander Constant. He a powerful businessman who is absolutely ruthless. This play is about choosing between good and evil. Theodore represents good and Alexander represents evil. Monica is playing the lead character, Cyndra Mckie, she has the same talents as these men but she's unsure of herself. Sometimes she wants to help others like Theodore. Sometimes she just wants to be selfish like Alexander. Both men want her because they both want her inherent strength, although for different reasons. Uh oh I think the scene now is the pivotal one Monica told me about. Monica is in a living room with both Theodore and Alexander. They want her to choose between them. They're both presenting their arguments.

Theodore: *Cyndra you know how I feel about you. You know we can be happy together. Together you and I can make a difference in this world.*

Alexander: *What can he offer you but stress? How much money is he making helping the poor?*

Cyndra: *Money isn't everything.*

Alexander: *You didn't say that when I flew us to Paris for two weeks. You didn't say that when I bought you all that jewelry. You said nothing when I paid your debts.*

Theodore: *You can't buy love.*

Alexander: *You can't live on it either. Money isn't everything, but it makes things go a lot easier. Cyndra you know this isn't about money. You know...I love you and would give a fortune to have you.*

Theodore: *What kind of life would you have with him? Everything he has done in his life has been for his self. He thinks the world is his playground. People are just toys to him. He uses everybody.*

Alexander: *You're right, I do think about myself. We all do. No matter how altruistic we claim to be. Everybody on this planet ultimately acts out of self-interest.*

Theodore: *Yes but my self-interest is at least making a difference in the lives of others.*

Cyndra: *I wish you two would stop. Both of you have good points. I enjoy what both of you have to offer but I can only be with one of you.*

Alexander: *So choose. This...man can't offer you a tenth of what I can offer.*

Theodore: *He's right Cyndra. I don't have his resources. Materially anyway. All I can offer is love and spiritual fulfillment. We can be complete with each other.*

Alexander: *You can be broke with each other. How long would your "love" last if bill collectors are calling or your car breaks down and you can't afford to fix it. How long will that "love" last then? Cyndra with me you will never want for anything.*

Theodore: *Yes you will have the material goodies but what will you have inside. What about your soul?*

Cyndra: *I...don't know.*

Theodore: *You have to choose Cyndra. You have to make the decision that is right for you.*

Alexander: *The decision should be to me. You know I'm right Cyndra.*

Cyndra: *I don't know what's right. Both of you pull at me. Both of you have so much to offer. I don't know which way to go. Which one to choose. I wish I did know. Both of you...I need time to make this decision. Can you respect that?*

Theodore: *Yes I can.*

Alexander: *Make the right decision.*

The stage goes dark for intermission. The second half of the play has Cyndra interacting with a lot of people as she is making her decision. At the end of the play Cyndra chooses Theodore which has everybody in the audience standing up and cheering wildly. I'm right there clapping like crazy. The cast got a standing ovation at the end of the play. Right now I'm waiting for Monica to come out. I hope she likes my surprise. Here she comes now.

"You were great." I pull a bouquet of roses from behind my back and hand them to Monica.

"Steve, these are so pretty. Thank you," Monica says with tears in her eyes as she hugs and kisses me on the cheek.

"I have some more surprises."

"You do?"

"Yes this will be a night of surprises."

****

"Dinner was great." Monica says as we walk along the Georgetown harbor holding hands. We had dinner at Marco's. Expensive as always. Chicken dinners that anyplace else would have cost $4.95. I didn't mind spending the money though. I'm enjoying Monica's company. During dinner Monica was telling me about all the craziness backstage before, during and after the show. As usual she had me dying. After dinner we decided to walk around the Georgetown Harbor. It's a beautiful night. Stars are out. Monica's looking beautiful. She has on a white dress that comes a little below her knees. I have on a light gray double breasted suit with very subtle pink and light green pinstripes. I've had this suit for years. Yet another suit that I had to take in when I lost the weight. This night is so perfect. We stop to look at the water. Monica looks out with a pleasant look on her face. I look out into the harbor and look back at Monica. Man, she's beautiful. She notices me staring and smiles.

"Why are you smiling? See something you like?" Monica asks playfully.

"You can say that. You're very beautiful,"

Monica laughs. "You're just noticing? I thought you needed glasses."

"Modest too. It's so endearing." I look into her eyes. They are so beautiful, especially at night.

"I think you're very handsome."

Wow she thinks I'm handsome. "Wow you think I'm handsome."

"I wouldn't be your friend otherwise."

"I've known that women were shallow."

"No, men are shallow. Women have taste."

"Oh excuse me."

"Yes women have great taste." Monica squeezes my hand. It sends a jolt through my body.

I move closer to her. "Men have great taste too."

"It's hard to tell sometimes," Monica says seductively.

"Not in this case." I pull her closer and kiss her lips lightly. She puts her arms around me and kisses harder. After about a minute we stop and pull away a bit, looking into each other's eyes as her hands are in mine. "We could be risking a great friendship."

"Or this could be the next step in a great love relationship. Something that will last a very long time," Monica says with a twinkle in her eye.

"Are you scared?"

"No. In life you have to have to go for it. Are you scared?"

"Not anymore."

"So where do we go from here?"

"How about we go back to my place?"

"Sounds good to me." Monica grabs and kisses me fiercely.

****

We arrive back at my building both anxiously anticipating the next few hours. This is going to be so nice. We park the car and go from the garage to the elevator to my floor. As we get off the elevator we almost run into Laura.

"Sorry about that Laura," I say.

Laura looks very depressed. "No problem Steve."

"Are you alright?"

"I...I'm okay."

"Laura this is Monica. Monica, Laura."

The two exchange greetings.

"Steve, thanks for everything," Laura says.

"No problem," I respond without thinking about what she said.

Laura gets on the elevator. "Goodbye,"

"That was weird," I say to Monica when the elevator door closed.

"What was weird?"

"I don't know." Odd the elevator is going up. Up!?!

I open my apartment door. "Monica, I'll be back in a second."

"What's going on?"

"I need to check on something."

"Okay," Monica says as she enters my apartment.

Something tells me that I'd better get up there quick. Come on, come on elevator. Alright here it is. Come on...Come on, alright, top floor. Gotta get to the roof. I hope she's not th...she's climbing the rail. "Laura!!! What the hell are you doing!?!"

"Steve leave me alone. This is my business."

At least she stops climbing. I can't blow this. "Laura what are you doing over there? Answer me!"

"What does it look like? I can't take this anymore. No friends. Jordan left me..."

"What about your parents?"

"My parents? My parents? My father left when I was a little girl. My mother always acted like she was jealous of me. I didn't have any brothers or sisters. I already told you about my uncles and cousins. I don't have anybody."

"You always have somebody even if it's just God."

"I never believed in God. My family wasn't into church.

"You can always start."

"I think it's too late. I don't know what to do. I don't know where to start. I don't even know if I want to start."

"Start from zero."

"What?"

"Start from zero. When everything seems like it's going wrong, you have to cut your losses and start from zero."

"I don't know if I can. I don't know if I have the strength."

"You have the strength. You just don't realize it."

"I don't have the strength, I'm weak."

I slowly move closer. "Laura, listen to me. You are not weak. The fact is you survived all of this time despite everything you said happened to you. You can do so much. Being a survivor makes you special."

"But it...was so hard. I was always alone."

"You won't be alone anymore. I'll be there for you. I promise."

"How can you promise that!?! You can't! What happens when I need to talk to you and you have to spend time with that girl downstairs?"

"I don't have to be your only friend. Stop being so damn introverted. Get involved in some things. You'll make more friends, you'll see."

"I tried. I'm tired of trying. I'm tired of being hurt. I'm tired of people acting like they're scared of me. I'm tired of people treating me like a freak of nature. I'm tired." Laura begins to climb.

"Laura what the hell are you doing!?!" I finally lose my patience. "You think you're the only one with problems!?! You think you're the only one who thinks that life has treated them unfairly!?! You think..."

"I know other people have had it tough but..."

"Don't interrupt me again!!! You know what!?!" I compose myself. "You look at me and think I got myself together but I'm not there. There was a time when I thought I was the man. Then I lost my job. I lost my friends. I went through a string of women. Had to move out of a big apartment. I went all the way down to zero. To zero!"

"H...how did you come back?"

"I prayed and I made a choice. I chose to rise. I refused to stay at zero. You have to make that choice."

"I don't know if I can. I need your help."

"Sorry, you have to make that choice yourself. I can't help you make the decision. Only after the decision can I help you."

"What's the point then? If you don't want to help..."

"That's right, take your own life. Nobody cares." God please guide me on this.

"What?"

"You heard me. If you want to choose to take your life that's your choice."

"Yo...You're not going to stop me?"

"No. You and only you have to make that choice."

"Steve, I..."

"Choose."

"But..."

"Choose."

"I..."

"Choose."

Laura steps away from the railing and walks towards me crying. "Help me,"

I put my arms around her. "I'll help you. I promise."

"Why are you so nice to me?"

"We're here to help each other."

"Thank you."

"You're welcome but if you really want to thank me, help somebody else in need."

"Okay."

"Now let's get down from here."

"Is it hard starting from zero?"

"Not at all. When you start from zero, you can only grow,"
I say and then chuckle.

"What's so funny?"

"I'm starting to sound like this brother named Darryl."

We went back to my apartment where Monica is waiting on
my couch with some soft music playing.

"Monica, I'm truly sorry about this but my neighbor Laura
is in a really bad way. She needs some company tonight. Laura
have a seat I'll make some tea."

"I'm sorry," Laura says as she sits down. "I didn't mean to
disturb anything it's just..." Laura buries her face in her hands and
starts crying.

Monica puts her arms around Laura. "Just let it go.
Whatever it is it'll be better."

"Monica's right." I sit at the other side of Laura.
"Everything will be alright."

"But I'm taking away from you two spending time
together," Laura says.

"Don't worry, Monica and I have plenty of time to be
together." I smile at Monica who smiles back in agreement.

Epilogue

Saturday night. Party at Joe's. I've been waiting for this party all week, especially after all that overtime I put into work. I love my job, but it was a rough week. Put in a lot of work for that auto accident case. The week is over though. Time to party. Shouldn't complain about work though. I do get paid well. I have a nice car. Nice build. I can't believe I was so big a couple of years ago. Now I look like I'm wasting away. Hey...somebody's knocking at the door.

"I'll get it," Monica says. She was waiting for me to get ready for the party. We have been together all day. We have spent a whole lot of time together these past couple of months.

Monica opens the door to greet Laura. "Hey girl."

"Hi Monica. You look nice. With that outfit on Steve might have some competition," Laura says as she came in, commenting on Monica's jeans, boots, and lightweight tennis shirt.

"You look good too Laura," Monica responds. Laura has on a skirt and matching top with some pumps.

I come out of the bathroom. "Hi Laura." I have on a polo shirt, jeans and loafers.

"Hi Steve," Laura smiles.

"Steve go back and finish dressing. We have a little while," Monica says as she and Laura give me that "we have girl talk" look. Ever since that night I talked Laura out of suicide and brought her back to my apartment her and Monica have been the best of friends. Sometimes Monica would come over to my apartment, drop her things off and go hang out with Laura. I guess that's good. Laura needed a female friend.

We leave the apartment about twenty minutes later. We go over to Ray and Ted's to pick them up. When we get there Monica gets out of the car to hug and kiss Ray and Ted. Monica and Ted then make goofy faces at each other. They had become instant friends since they met a month or so ago. Personally I think that they were brother and sister in a past life the way they clicked. Monica makes a point of introducing Ted to Laura. Monica's always looking out for people. After everybody gets in the car, we head on to Joe's for the party. Now with five people in the car things can get a bit lively.

"How come you fellas don't get a car?" I ask Ray and Ted.

"I'm just getting out of school man. Give me another month," Ray responds, laid back as ever.

"What I need a car for when I have you," Ted says. "That's the only reason I'm your friend. That and to laugh at your head."

"Hey Ted that's why I'm his girlfriend," Monica says. "But you have to leave my baby's head alone. If you don't I'm going to have to hurt you."

"That'll be the day," Ted laughs.

"You guys are crazy," Laura says to Ted more than anybody else.

"You don't know half of it," Ted says looking into Laura eyes.

"Hey Ted," Monica says. "You see that movie on cable last night, *He Gets His*? Was it corny or what?"

"You watched it?"

"I had to knock Steve out last night for saying something smart so I had to nothing else to do."

"That movie was bad. Looked like it was made by someone using an old movie camera and it was financed by a garage sale."

"I wouldn't give it that much credit. The fact that the main character was a player was bad enough. His stomach was poking all out, cheeks fat, he looked like he smelled. I wonder how he got the part."

"He was probably the director's cousin."

"Can you two ever watch a movie without critiquing it?" I ask Monica and Ted.

"No!" Monica and Ted say together.

We all laugh.

****

This party is nice. Not as wild as the last time. As soon as we get to Joe's, Ted and Laura head right to the food. Man they look like they clicked. All the women head for Ray. Everybody chilled and talked. More mingling and laughing than the last time. Monica is having a good time. I'm amazed at how many brothers are hitting on her when we're not standing together. Every time though she points them to me. I overheard one say, "We can still be friends right?" That cracks me up. Like he approached her to be her friend. It's good just to chill out at the party. Somebody touches my shoulder.

"Steve?" Tamara says looking the same as she did a couple of years ago.

"In the flesh."

"Steve you look good. I cannot believe how much weight you have lost."

"I've been working out."

"I see, I see. So what else have you been doing?"

"Well right now I'm working for Joe. I'm about to take the GRE's in a little while."

"Decided to go to grad school huh?"

"Oh yes. Have to expand my mind."

"So what are you going for?"

"I'm not entirely sure. I leaning towards getting a Ph.D. in African-American history. It's something I really enjoy."

"Good for you."

"I was thinking about law school for a while but there are too many attorney's out there and not enough dedicated teachers. That'll be my way of helping other people."

Tamara moves closer to me. "That is real nice Steve. You know, I think about you a lot,"

"You do?"

"Yes I do. I think I might have been too hard on you. I think I should have given you more of a chance."

"Really?" I'm try to hide my amusement.

"Yes really. I was thinking...maybe we should get together later on. After the party. We could go back to my place. Relax and see what happens," Tamara says in a low and seductive voice.

"Sounds nice, but I'm busy tonight."

"Maybe later."

"Maybe never. Monica...can you come here for a second," I call across the room to where Monica was talking with Ted and Laura.

"Tamara, this is my lady Monica." I introduce Monica to Tamara.

"Nice to meet you," Monica says cheerfully.

"Likewise," Tamara says weakly.

"How ya like me now?" Ted says loudly as he and Laura walk by with a plate of chicken wings.

Monica stifles a laugh. I manage to keep a straight face.

The rest of the night we all laugh and have a good time. I really enjoy myself. The past couple of years have been rough, but I survived. I survived and prospered. I went to zero and I came back up. I'm spiraling.

About the Author

Who is Rom Wills? I have had many words used to describe me. I've been called mysterious, brilliant, and goofy. I'm the type of person who can read a comic book in the morning and an obscure book on deep metaphysics in the evening. I can hang out on a street corner one moment and with powerful movers and shakers the next. I can talk about the read option offense in pro football and the inner workings of the national economy the next. I can say without conceit that I could star in some "Most Interesting Man in the World" commercials. I'm formally educated with advanced degrees and yet my best education has come from simply living life. There are very few things I haven't either personally experienced or know someone who has experienced certain things. My life would make a very compelling movie.

So who is Rom Wills? I'm a man who is on a mission to make a difference in the lives of the people I touch. Everything that I have experienced in life, good and bad, has been a life lesson. Through my writings, lectures, workshops, or talking trash in a barbershop I strive to share something that will positively impact the people around me.

Rom Wills is the author of the international bestseller Nice Guys and Players and the follow-up Sexual Chemistry.

Follow Rom on the World Wide Web:

www.romwills.com

Facebook.com/Willspublishing

Twitter: @RomWills1

IG: @Romwills

www.ingramcontent.com/pod-product-compliance
Lightning Source LLC
Chambersburg PA
CBHW021950010726
47494CB00003B/666